TALES OF THE MER FAMILY ONYX

Mermaid stories on land and under the sea

by

Susan I. Weinstein

Pelekinesis
NEW EDITIONS

TALES OF THE MER FAMILY ONYX:
Mermaid stories on land and under the sea by Susan I. Weinstein

ISBN-13: 978-1-938349-54-6
eISBN: 978-1-938349-55-3
Library of Congress Control Number: 2017939968

Cover design and illustration
    by Susan I. Weinstein and Mark Givens

Interior illustrations by Susan I. Weinstein

First Pelekinesis Printing 2017
For information:
Pelekinesis Publishing Group,
112 Harvard Ave #65, Claremont, CA 91711 USA

Pelekinesis PUBLISHING GROUP
www.pelekinesis.com

TALES OF THE MER FAMILY ONYX

Mermaid stories on land and under the sea

Susan I. Weinstein

This book is dedicated to Charlie, who inspired me to make up these stories— once upon a time. And to Carl, who listened to them, as they changed over the miles until we reached the seashore.

A MODERN CLASSIC FOR CHILDREN
by Sonia Taitz, author of *Great with Child*

The Tales of the Mer Family Onyx are nothing short of spectacular. The author has created a beautiful and convincing alternative world—a modern-day Oz or Thousand Acre Wood. The stories of this mermaid family are engaging, imaginative, and gorgeously written and wisely resolved. Each chapter presents an adventure involving the children of the Mer Family, who rule the undersea world. From the powerful and majestic Neptune to the smallest mer baby, each character comes alive and will appeal to children of all ages, whether male or female. What a joy to find a new classic like this in our fast-paced, modern world!

FOR ALL THE MERMAID LOVERS
by Lara Steensland Mullarkey, Integrated Early Childhood Program, Teachers College, Columbia University

If you have a child who loves mermaids and mer families, this is the book for you. Each chapter makes the perfect bedtime read aloud for younger children. Together the chapters weave a full mer-world.

EVOCATIVE MERMAID STORIES, GREAT FOR KIDS AND ADULTS TOO
by Susan R. Chalfin, author of *Remember You Will Die*, from Fresh Slices

A wonderfully evocative adventure story, great for kids of all ages—and adults will enjoy it too. An adventurous family of Mer-children compete to explore new worlds, from the land of miniature mermaids—where they discover their half-sister Pinky, to a colony of prehistoric humans to today's Mermaid Day Parade on Coney Island. Their enchanting undersea universe is described in lively and colorful prose, with generous splashes of humor.

CHARMING AND INSIGHTFUL...DIVE IN

by Ann Schwartz, Former Copy Chief Grand Central Publishing,
President at Fantastic Flexagons

These tales are charming with the kinds of details children love. We learn about the food, pets, modes of transportation, gardens, and homes under the sea. I loved the way each child in the mermaid family represents a different personality type. There is a child for everyone to identify with. And the basic need of children: to push their parents' limits and to explore beyond what is "allowed" is honored, and King Neptune and his wife understand that. The different chapters and adventures are imaginative and fun and the love between the different family members, including the cute miniature mermaid, binds them all. Each adventure presents a different kind of danger/entanglement that the mer-chlld or children must extricate themselves from. But again, I think the author's understanding of the need for a child to have secrets that his parents don't know about—a life away from them—that makes this book stand out. The chapter that weaves our reality with the mermaids' and introduces a human boy who goes to the Coney Island Mermaid Parade is the one of the books outstanding examples of that. I recommend this book to all children who love fantasy adventure AND their parents. It's a real pearl!

LOVED THIS BOOK!!

by David Goldman, DG Media Agency

My entire family was happily surprised and treated to an amazing story full of original characters and beautiful descriptive writing. Susan Weinstein has created a world here which has all of the potential to become the next great world class fantasy hit. I only hope she is working on a follow up book as this is being written. I highly recommend this for ages 4 and up-the adults loved it too!

Contents

Preface to the New Edition

Tales of the Mer Family Onyx started with stories I made up on trips from New York City to a family beach cottage in Long Beach Island, New Jersey. My son and I developed a storytelling habit, because we had followed the Surgeon General's guidelines about no screens before age two. And it entertained both of us. About halfway into the journey, when he was not yet sleepy, he would tell me what characters he wanted and sometimes what happened. He was greatly taken with mermaids, so there were stories about bad mermaids, lobsters, a giant baby, a sea witch, a dragon and many disasters. I would improvise, but the details counted and, like a good director, he would tell me if I was going in the wrong direction. I knew I was on the right track, when with a smile he would drift into what I thought was sleep. But if I stopped, a skeptical eye would open, as though to say, 'Is that the ending?'

Eventually our stories evolved into the creation of a whole Mer family. Many young children admire older ones, so we had boy and girl tween twins, Bowrain and Rainbow, girl teen twins, Emerald and Sapphire. Wild baby Ruby was great fun and there was intrigue around the sensitive mini-mermaid, Pinky. Our Neptune had powerful – vacillating moods. He was here one minute, gone the next in a job which took him all over the planet. The mainstay of the Mer Family was the all-seeing, thoughtful Glendora. Both kind and demanding, she sometimes could be a source of annoyance for her children.

Fantasy is a passage to the adult world and it can be a

way to cope, when children are confronted with it. My son was three and a half when he saw the plane go into the first tower. He did one drawing, where the plane went into the tower, and one where it did not—the pilot changed his mind. He liked that one better. Life was still fluid with fantasy, though the division between nature and humans became clear. He pointed out trash on the beach, dead fish washed up with plastic, tar that stuck to his bare feet. In Florida, he could not swim in the ocean because of red algae, caused by global warming and chemicals. A local TV station stopped us and videotaped his thoughts on the red algae, encouraging him to puzzle out the world.

He knew mermaids weren't real but even at age five, really wanted to meet one. This was no contradiction. He thought maybe he was wrong. "Who knows?" A year older, he wanted a story where a real mermaid met a fake one at the Coney Island Mermaid Parade. He was in that parade with green skin, proudly carrying a red trident. I wore a vinyl material printed with a coral reef. We walked the boards with our own kind, human Mer people.

Of course, about age 9 or 10, Jersey Devils, ghosts and werewolves became more interesting than mermaids. We had screens with images; Tim Burton's Jack Skellington and the bride from *The Corpse Bride* and in my son's early teens, after seeing a stage revival, *Carrie.* In the years when science merged with fantasy, my son made shrunken heads and Fiji Mermaids. He was still exploring magical creatures, though darker ones. Magical creatures, a bridge between these worlds, eventually merged into a vocation for him.

Not only children seek to know the world and where they fit in. That is probably why Mer stories are found in many cultures, though bottoms are sometimes water snakes not fish. Mer folk can be male or female, virtuous or evil succubi/incubi. Do they intentionally lure sailors to death in the deep, or are they well-meaning innocents, amoral in the way of elemental spirits? Like nature, Mer has both sides. Stories perhaps reflect mankind's unease with the untamable.

The focus of *Tales of The Mer Family Onyx* was to explore and have fun. There are ninjas and mini mermaids, as well as magical devices, tridents that change size, shell phones and a basin that facilitates travel between time and worlds. But, when I started to write these stories down, at my husband's suggestion, the logic of our fantasy world seemed most important. I had read and studied fantasy classics, such as L. Frank Baum's *The Sea Fairies* and all fourteen *Oz* books, E. Nesbit's *The Magic City*, *The Amulet* and others. Nesbit was an inspiration to both Baum and C.S.Lewis. Her understanding of the intersection of magic and science, how imaginative logic works in children and adults is extraordinary.

After our work week, the Mer Family Onyx restored our silliness and wonder. Somewhat fitting our collaboration, my son was an occasional critic, especially useful in his teen years. I revised with and without him to make this book of a magical family, who act as stewards of the seas, arbiters of a kind of " Better Coral Reefs and Ocean Gardens." I tried to recapture our sense of discovery of the *Onyx* world.

Tales of the Mer Family Onyx is intended, like the Baum and Nesbit classics, to be a "family book." The idea was children of mixed age groups being read to by a parent. There are elements in these stories for young children, who may relate to baby Ruby's adventures. There is a narrative meant for adults that kids may not understand. That's okay. Every day kids puzzle out the adult world. They can ask the reader what a word or idea means or look it up. And where an older child may be impatient with details young children enjoy, there's the headstrong teenaged Sapphire.

For a child, hearing a book read aloud is different than reading alone on a screen. For instance, consider the *Oz* books. In *Glinda of Oz,* there's a chapter about war between the Flatheads and the Squeezers that was perfect to explain why countries go to war, when my son saw news of the war in Iraq. It turned out Baum's story was an allegory to explain the first World War and dictators. That war was over in 1918, and this last Oz book was published in 1920.

I hope readers will find similar parables in our mermaid world. Know the family is pagan, as elemental spirits may be, but very moral. Some values are my son, the critic's. He knew very young that creatures were eaten for food and so endangered. In his teens, he thought the book too "adult" but still loved willful wild Ruby, the tender sensitivity of Pinky, Emerald and Sapphire's teen blues. Most of all, he related to the sass of Bowrain and Rainbow's tween rivalry.

I hope adults and children experience joy, discovery, recognition, sweetness, fantasy and— a good night's sleep.

S.W.

AND *in the basin saw the mermaid cleaning the anemone beds in her beloved garden.*

PROLOGUE

As Glendora Onyx gazed into her silver basin thinking of her husband, Neptune, the opaque water cleared. There was Neptune, head in the clouds, tail firmly on ocean bottom. He stretched his arms to the heavens and electricity shot from his fingers, charging the atmosphere. On his face was a smile of complete happiness. Loves making storm clouds, thought Glendora with humorous affection and a touch of awe.

The Merqueen put the basin down and repositioned herself on a huge clamshell, where she could see out the window of the Coral Castle. With the movement, her tail shimmered from turquoise to deepest purple and reverse. For a moment, she watched sunlight seep to the depths as eel lights went out, signaling a new day.

Glendora brushed her burgundy hair, until it gleamed with orange highlights. She checked her face in a mirror held in place by living coral. I look very well for a mermaid of four thousand years she thought. Are the kids up and about?

She reached again for the silver basin and saw her daughter Emerald getting baby Ruby her bottle of sea cow milk, then opening Pinky's oyster shell.

At three hundred fifty years, Ruby was a bit old for a bottle, mused Glendora. She watched Pinky's tiny body swimming onto the baby mermaid's nose; heard the tinkling laugh of a mini mermaid and happy baby shrieks. Emerald, her deep sea green eyes full of amusement, kneeled to offer Pinky transport to the conch shell in which she took her morning bath.

Right on schedule, of course. Glendora approved the way Emerald took charge, though she expected nothing less from her dependable first born. She whispered "Sapphire," the name of Emerald's twin, and in the basin saw the mermaid cleaning the anemone beds in her beloved garden. Glendora sang out, "Can you bring me some fresh dew and seaweed for cakes?" Sapphire scraped her long golden trident against a rock to remove some barnacles. She tied back her thick blue-black hair with a glow squirmy. "No problem, mom. Long as you behave," she said, a twinkle in her electric blue eyes.

"And when do I not?" Glendora twinkled back. She allowed Sapphire her rebellion now and then. Sapphire was almost sixteen hundred, the age you begin to think about who you are besides a child of your parents.

(Around that same age, Neptune had begun his courtship.) Since they weren't formally introduced, Glendora nodded but took little notice, while he probed more rocks. "Lava boulders," he explained. With those rocks, also covered with coral, he formed a crude circle a short distance away. Glendora appeared not to see but she noticed immediate growth. A future coral reef, she thought. Gazing into her farseeing mirror, she reflected on life—the nothing that is everything—as mermaids do. All the while, she observed the enterprising merman.

Besides the coral, Neptune was enchanting Glendora.

Since mermaids love a good story, he told her of his interest in living construction, where materials and creator worked together.

She watched fascinated, as he formed the foundation of what would become the Coral Castle. He planted two halves of a ship and, when the circular reef was almost solid, used mainsail poles to encourage the coral to grow upward. Supports for floors would follow.

At Neptune's request, the living coral descended from exterior ledges and adhered to circular tunnels of plant material curved inside the structure. These became swim ways leading to flexible rooms with floating walls, like Bowrain and Rainbow's suite or bubble rooms like Ruby and Pinky's.

With the interior in place, Neptune froze a lightning bar and sculpted coral reefs into the smooth shape of a Nautilus shell. By then, Glendora shyly admitted that she would like to become his Merqueen and live in this Coral Castle. Neptune promised she would be mistress of the castle and his heart.

He bowed to her in most things, though of course not when he disagreed. And she sweetly acknowledged that she would seek his counsel, except when she kept her own.

Because the Coral Castle was made of living organisms, it responded not only to Neptune's orders but to the emotions of the inhabitants of the castle.

Sometimes the pink coral took on a dark rose hue, responding to tempers or sadness, or a white hue of happy exclamations—the joys of the noisy Onyx family. Room to grow, thought Neptune with satisfaction. Though now and then, for fun, he made typhoon shaped rooms or whole corridors like the interior of a whale. He couldn't resist tinkering, though others had to ask permission for changes.

And the one room that never changed was his office and adjoining conference room.

From his perch on a scavenged captain's throne, he viewed a map of the incremental adjustments made throughout the castle. Outside, whales, fierce fighting fish and lethal squids protected the Coral Castle from stray explorers. Within, Glendora grew enchantments in Sapphire's gardens to protect the tiny creatures that continually repaired and rebuilt her family's home.

Not long after, Neptune and the lovely Glendora of the burgundy hair were formally joined by an elder of her clan. They exchanged living fin jewels and family tridents. And in good time welcomed their first Merbabes into the sea world. Neptune was so proud, a merbabe on each arm.

One baby had tufts of bright green hair, the other's was bright blue. The eyes of Emerald, the green haired one, calmly reflected sea water, while Sapphire's opened with electric surprise. Flapping around Neptune's wrists were baby tails of electric blue and chartreuse. "The tails will darken," said Glendora knowingly.

"Now where did you last see the nursery?"

That floating nursery would be vacated years before another set of mertwins were born. Rainbow, a mermaid and Bowrain, a merboy were quite good at wriggling out of their rocking clams and paddling to their parents' billowy suite, slipping into the undulating water bed. This morning, looking into the magical basin, Glendora was annoyed to see these same mertwins, at eleven – hundred-years old, still asleep in their own waterbeds.

Snail alarm again not set, thought Glendora, annoyed. She placed her mouth close to the water and emitted high pitched peels of alarm. As the waves of sound reverberated into the twins' room, Bowrain sat up, as did Rainbow. "It's that time again," said Rainbow. "Don't I know it," said Bowrain. "Guess we might as well get up." "Merschool," said Rainbow, "sounds like a bad idea to me!"

Bowrain was already out of bed, swinging his tail to their stream room. Rolling over and over he dislodged debris from his scales. Then, Bowrain used the tentacle floss Dr. Murk had given him. Take that, jelly termites, he thought, fearing new holes in his teeth from the sweet jellies he consumed only yesterday. He would do better today!

Rainbow opened her oysters and took out a perfect pearl for each ear. She attached them to her lobes with mermaid stickum and looked for her uniform. Merschool let them wear pearls or decorative creatures, but everyone had to wear the same blue Mertunic boy or maid. At least the maid ones were form fitting and didn't bulge when she swam. It bore the trident shape, Neptune's logo, which made her feel proud. All the Onyx children wore a trident charm on a chain around their necks. But she was the only merprincess at school and everyone knew it!

Superior is as superior does, thought Glendora to her most headstrong daughter. I trust your homework is done?

Rainbow grumbled. "Did I give you permission to spy

in my room?"

"When you get up by yourself, I will stay out of your room. I could use the beauty sleep," said Glendora sharply. "See you both at breakfast."

Glendora let the waters return to opaque. There were dried sea plant cereals and sea cow milk to get ready and Neptune's favorite power drink, charged by eel from Java.

When they were all on their way, she would help Emerald with her charges. Ruby and Pinky could be a finful. Once they were in their routines, Glendora could think about her day, as it formed around her.

The Coral Castle was a love song from her husband and never a better poem did a mermaid have. Pinkish walls were different every day, like her melodies and their lives. The only constant was their love and work, and the pleasure they took in both. It was now time to begin again.

Glendora swam to the nursery, humming a song about plants with deep roots at the bottom of the sea, whose tops grew upward to the sky. As the plants broke the surface, she swam through the bubbly doorway of the nursery to greet Emerald.

Pinky was playing happily with Ruby, so perhaps Emerald might help her make seaweed cakes and dew drink? Or perhaps they could swim near the surface, harvest floating plants, warmed by the sun?

Neptune roamed the seas of the world, but was always in residence at the Coral Castle. From the time Glendora gave him her heart, he was able to see his household wherever the wind took him. Being married to a mermaid he was never alone.

Glendora went to work. With two sets of twins, her baby and her adopted daughter Pinky, she had to recreate order on a daily basis. Everyone knew their role in the household and she was very strict, especially with the wayward Rainbow. She and Bowrain needed her strong direction. How would they find their way out of and back to the Coral Castle, if she didn't direct them?

Rainbow Onyx, Bowrain behind her, swam past the curving corridors that led to her parents chambers. Through their rooms she swam swiftly. The curve of the walls became more rounded, until she arrived at the center of the Coral Castle. What would she find inside that small interior curl? Every time, her mother snagged her before she could enter. Now she was again halted by Glendora's omnipresence. "Get to school!"

CHAPTER 1

Glendora's Silver Basin

Bowrain Onyx knew he had no business in his mother's private sanctum, the inner curl of that castle. Yet here he was, holding her mysterious silver basin. The ever – changing surface was as fascinating as the iridescent liquid inside. And it was bottomless! Once Bowrain saw Glendora's whole body follow her hand into its depths.

He ran into her empty room and glanced inside the basin startled to see a young Glendora, a saucy mermaid with deep burgundy hair decorated with huge pink orchids. One minute she winked at him, the next his adult mother stood beside him, explaining why he should not get too close to the interior.

"You might fall in and not be able to get out. And you'll disturb the ether."

"What's that?"

"The stuff between our time and another, a kind of wall made of something like gas. When you're older, I'll teach you about ether and time travel."

How much older, wondered Bowrain, who like his twin sister, Rainbow, was 1100 years old. Grown-ups always said "when you're older" to put kids off, but he respected Glendora's wishes. His mom did know more than him, much as he didn't like to admit it. But today, she would excuse his trespass. After all, it was for science.

Excitedly, Bowrain pulled out his treasure, a reddish stone etched with lines and cavities, an ancient fossil. He ran his finger over it, considering how it looked like a fish and an animal.

Maybe an ancestor of the Mer, and he had made the discovery! Neptune would be so proud if he brought it back! Bowrain would make sea history, adding to the wonder of all creatures under the water.

With pride Bowrain remembered finding the fossil in the stalls below the Coral Castle where the seahorses were stabled. He had fed Boy Boy and Guy Guy their sea oats and was replacing the old kelp when he saw the stone embedded in the sand.

Throw the stone into the silver basin, he thought. Maybe a live creature will swim back. He was about to release it, when he saw his reflection in Glendora's abalone mirror. It was like being caught in the act, though the only person he saw was a mischievous-looking merboy, with greenish blonde hair and eyes like turquoise.

He bobbed, admiring his sleekly shining tail—ranging backward in a colorful spectrum from black blue to a yellow white—thinking what a silly he was. Glendora would not return until this evening.

She and Emerald, his older sister, were helping Neptune finish enchantments to seal some bad caves in their cove. Sapphire, Emerald's twin, was working in the anemone garden, and baby Ruby and tiny Pinky were still abed.

Happily, pesky Rainbow was gone. Her seahorse, Guy Guy was missing from the stable. For once Bowrain didn't have to share an adventure—or his fossil. He found it, so it was his, none of this twin business of claiming half ownership.

Bowrain knelt by the basin and opened his hand. As the stone hit the water, a huge suction drew him inside the basin. He was an astonished tiny creature seeking a hold, pulled downward through iridescent silver and pink.

He flopped hard on yellow earth and flipped onto his stomach sniffing the air. No water, he thought grimly, no savannah, unless you count that sparse clump of grass. "What could be worse?" he asked before his twin fell on top of him.

"Rainbow!" he gasped.

"You were up to something with that fossil." "Can't I have my own adventure?"

"Fine with me," said Rainbow, a bit miffed, "Where's home?"

"You only know you're in an adventure," Bowrain recited in his best Neptune voice, "once you're out of it."

"Just like dad!" Rainbow rolled her eyes. "Think BEFORE you do something. Wish I had." She felt her tail with some concern, "Too hot. And we can't move. Good choice, Bro."

"I assumed water," said Bowrain, annoyed since he hadn't exactly invited her along. Shading his eyes against the sun's glare, he saw ahead what looked like a glittering pool and two small figures.

"Mirage," Rainbow pronounced. Bowrain called "Mirage, mirage! Come out wherever you are!"

The Onyx Mertwins laughed, as the distant figures turned in their direction. Two children, a boy and girl scampered toward Bowrain and Rainbow. They were a dark brown hue, underscored by the identical cloths they wore of spotted animal hide, sun bleached almost white. Both had tightly curled black hair, upturned noses, round mouths and golden hazel eyes wide with curiosity. They sat on their haunches and stared at the mertwins.

They're not just staring at the fish tails, Bowrain observed. Rainbow completed his thought,"But really the mystery of one set of twins meeting another! Do we look so alike? Bowrain dismissed this, "I'm handsome and you," Rainbow prepared to jab him with her nearest fin, "Are even more beautiful." she finished.

Rainbow preened as she spoke, and indeed her show – off gesture impressed the savannah boy, who bashfully looked at the ground.

She was indeed beautiful. Her yellow green hair had a hint of burgundy and her turquoise eyes were jewel bright.

Her tail ranged from lemon yellow to a deep royal blue. Like the princess she was, Rainbow gestured to the savannah boy that he could touch her tail. After the savannah girl's shy look, Bowrain let her do the same.

The savannah girl made a makeshift broom of grass and cleared off some of the dust from her imperial tail.

Bowrain thought the dust was the least of it. He pointed

urgently at the sun and the girl talked with her twin in their clicking language. Then the one savannah twin picked up Rainbow by the tail and dragged her over the powdery earth. Rainbow gagged on the stuff, feeling suffocated as it coated her tail. She yelled, "Where are they taking me?" Bowrain saw a pond and didn't mind being dragged.

Once at the small pond, the girl trickled water over Rainbow's scales. It was warm but wet, and Rainbow thought, no complaints, as the savannah girl carefully maneuvered her tail into the water. And soon Bowrain was beside her, sufficiently recovered, to draw a fossil with a stick in the sand.

One savannah twin burst into laughter, then the other. They seemed to find it hysterically funny and Rainbow and Bowrain wanted to be let in on the joke. Once the laughter subsided, the savannah twins waded around the rock which hid the stream's source underground. The girl extracted some kernels of grain hidden in the dusty ground on a small incline from the water's edge.

Then both sets of twins waited, passed the time by drawing in the sand, first with finger, then with a stick. Both knew tick tack toe but were getting bored, when several fish emerged from the spring. Trout, thought Bowrain, disappointed as they swam around the rock.

A fish tried to waddle up the shore after the crumbs. All the twins laughed, so comical was this fish trying to walk on four stubby legs.

"Like thick gills," Rainbow spoke to Bowrain in Mer, and the fish, surprised, answered in words familiar but different. "The fish is frustrated," said Rainbow. "He wants more crumbs and to eat savannah grass." The savannah twins looked from her to the fish, astounded, wanting to understand. Bowrain imitated the fish, pulling himself up the shore. The children laughed. Still, he felt a little sorry for the fish, sprawled on the shore.

"It's struggling to breath," said Rainbow, intuiting his thought.

Then Bowrain had an idea, it wouldn't really be messing with time, he thought, since he knew the outcome already. "Fish," said Bowrain. "Why land?"

"Hungry" was the gasping answer from the fish. "Dive into the stream, go back underground until the water is large," said Bowrain.

"Eat tiny krill, sea vegetables" said Rainbow.

The fish looked longingly at the land, replying in his ancient Mer, "Many creatures are walking out of the water."

"Go back!" said the mertwins, and the tiny gold tridents they wore on their necks glistened in the sun. The fish took it as a royal command. He flopped back into the water, swam to the source and disappeared. Others continued their futile uphill trek.

That one will survive now, thought the mertwins.

Bowrain picked up his stone and noticed the fossil was gone! He showed Rainbow and the savannah twins, who marveled at the strange trick. Then, tails comfortably in the water, the Onyx children splashed each other and took turns giving rides to the savannah twins. They were resting when the sun made its descent downward.

The girl drew a picture of Rainbow with the stick in the

yellow dirt.

Rainbow said, "Mermaid."

The girl repeated, "Mermaid" and thumped her stick, pointing to Rainbow.

"Your name?" Bowrain translated

"I'm Rainbow," Rainbow said.

The girl repeated, "I'm Rainbow."

Rainbow pointed to herself. "Rainbow." Then she took the stick and drew a picture of the girl. "You?"

The name the girl uttered sounded like a click. Bowrain gestured again and saw she did it with her tongue. He made a click also and she was delighted he knew her name. Then he drew a picture of the boy and pointed. The boy's name was a fierce sound. He imitated some kind of growling animal to show the Onyx children what he meant. Bowrain drew a merboy and said "Bowrain."

So engrossed were the children that they didn't notice a woman holding an empty jug. So shocked was she at the sight of Rainbow and Bowrain, she fell to her knees and bowed her head.

Neptune's children were used to adoration, but they felt embarrassed as more people came to gawk. Two men hoisted them on their shoulders and carried them away from the pond. They began to protest but the happy smiles of their new friends reassured them. In the center of a group of huts made from the yellow grass, was a platform with low chairs covered with rich animal skins.

The mertwins were carefully escorted onto the platform.

The savannah twins rested their fins in large gourds filled with water. Side by side, Rainbow and Bowrain greeted villagers, who came forward and bowed.

Each time, a savannah twin handed them a dipper filled with water and one of the mertwins would pour water on the petitioner's hands. Hungrily, they drank and were refreshed.

Thirsty work, thought Rainbow, and more boring than her father's court. She put her dipper aside and thrust her whole face into the welcome wetness. Bowrain shared her opinion and wondered if a fresh seaweed dinner was out of the question, as tribal members returned with an array of foods. There was little appeal in mush of some pulpy texture, but they politely tried it after watching the savannah twins contentedly eating with their fingers. The dried meat they wouldn't touch. The savannah twins consulted with the adults. The girl drew fish in dirt and looked inquiring. Both mertwins shouted, "No way!"

She looked perplexed. The savannah boy rubbed his tummy, making an inquiry. Then Rainbow pulled grass out of the platform and put it into the water. When it was wet, she chewed. The crowd clapped but Bowrain looked at her, "Are you really eating that?"

"Giving them a hint!" Rainbow said indignantly. Then tired and not a little hungry, the mertwins put their arms around each other, wondering how they would survive this place. The savannah twins noted their distress. They brought in a washtub with a fish. Once the horrified mertwins realized the fish was an interpreter not dinner, they talked eagerly. The fish, who understood the language of the savannah people as well as ancient Mer, had many questions about Neptune's kingdom. He also told them that the tribe thought they had come from the water spirit. Long had they prayed for rain.

Because of the drought, animals were dying of thirst, crops had dried, and humans suffered fear along with their thirst.

"I get it! We're supposed to act like gods."

Bowrain closed his eyes, as though in prayer. Rainbow pretended to do the same but peeked through her hands.

The villagers were muttering words and cries, accompanied by drumming and piping sounds from flutes of animal horn.

The water spirit was well-known to Bowrain and Rainbow. To contact him they needed no words. As the night quieted, they became aware of a subtle vibration from their tridents. Glendora missed them and wanted them home. They could picture their family sitting around the table, recounting their day and wondering what had become of the twins.

Neptune might have begun a search. Bowrain shrank to think of this. When his father learned about the basin, he would not be in a good humor. A fearsome force was Neptune's temper and Bowrain didn't want to inspire it! The village slept, including the savannah twins, who lay on a spotted animal skin at a respectful distance from their new friends.

In the distance minutes after dawn, the twins saw the conical shape of a giant tidal wave. Dad, thought Rainbow, as the unbelievable wave rolled through the savannah at a breathtaking pace. Quickly, the mertwins woke the savannah twins. Soon the rest of the tribe was out of the path of the wave.

The wall of water approached the Onyx children's platform and Bowrain called out, "Don't drown the village. It's my fault." Suddenly, water stopped moving across land. It climbed into the sky, a vertical column of revolving water. Gradually, it bent toward the site of the underground spring. Bowrain, with the girl on his back, and Rainbow, with the boy clinging to her tail, were swept up in the water. Diving and riding, they poured themselves into the overwhelmed pond.

The savannah twins were gasping, as uncomfortable in the water as the mertwins were in their dusty land. Rainbow and Bowrain kissed the savannah twins so they could breathe underwater. All were swept underground in the huge torrent. Now tiny, they passed through Glendora's basin, and found themselves on the floor of her bedroom in the Coral Castle. The red fossil stone clattered out with them, quickly palmed by Bowrain.

Glendora was brushing her long silver-streaked burgundy hair with a shell brush, when she noticed the four children on the floor. She looked from one set of twins to the other, amused. "Where are you from?" she asked the savannah children. To their surprise, they understood her words and poured out their story of finding the "water God twins" and about the funny walking fish.

"You are vegetarian?" asked Glendora.

The savannah twins said they ate grain mostly and meat

when available. Hunters of their tribe prayed to animal spirits and thanked them for letting the tribe survive. The twins pointed to their spotted skins and said they were very prized. The girl sadly squeezed hers and water ran out. "Heavy with water," she said.

Then Glendora spoke to the mertwins, who went to Sapphire's anemone garden. They returned with garments of living sea plants, ticklish but delightful to swim in.

Glendora gave the children delicious kelp sticks and sea vegetable chips with squid ink dip. Much revived, the savannah twins had many excited questions. "Are you people, creatures or gods?"

Glendora laughed, "All three. We're Mer."

"Older than your people," Rainbow added. "But we're not human. We're ourselves."

Glendora sighed, "We live in the between times."

"Timeless," Bowrain explained "Let me show you the rest of our Coral Castle. The reefs are constantly being rebuilt."

"They're alive," Rainbow added.

The African twins, enjoying their new ability to swim, kept up with Bowrain and Rainbow on a tour of the anemone gardens, the orchestra of clams and lobsters and the fish tapestry-makers, who used many-layered schools to form a constant motion of patterns and textures.

They learned about the worlds at different depths, sea folk personalities, age-old rivalries, predators and clowns.

When they returned to the Castle, Glendora gave them

platters of fresh krill and seaweed cakes. All were full and happy, when she gently explained that it was time for their guests to return home to their time. To each savannah twin she gave a sweet of candied plant jelly. With the jelly, she explained, they could continue to swim underwater until they reached land.

Glendora tilted her basin. As each child put a foot in, they vanished below the rim. Rainbow and Bowrain peered downward. They could see the now very tiny savannah twins, who asked them to come and play again soon. Waving, then splashing, the twins were visible in the little pond in their yellow landscape. When they emerged, they were surprised to be clothed in dry animal skins.

Bowrain placed his red stone in the basin to see what would happen. The stone went down in a vortex of water. It disappeared and a fish emerged from the pond! They'll never learn, those fish, thought Bowrain.

"Nor should they," said Glendora. "It's the will of some to walk and others to swim—their destiny."

Sad at leaving their new friends and tired from adventuring, Rainbow and Bowrain were swimming back to their room when Glendora called after them.

"Bowrain, Rainbow!" said Glendora, her hair floating in burgundy clouds around her, "You cannot use my basin without permission." The twins slowed, feeling contrite.

"I'm afraid this isn't the first time. For the worry you've caused me and the risk to Father Time, your actions must have consequences! You will help your sister today, tired or not." Bowrain and Rainbow groaned simultaneously. "Sapphire Onyx is weeding the garden and no complaints!"

Rainbow pursed her mouth. "I know it wasn't your idea," said Glendora to her daughter, "but you chose to go along."

"Could she be any stricter?" Bowrain grumbled, as he led Rainbow outside the Castle, where the gorgeous anemone garden was being tended by Sapphire Onyx. She had the iridescent thumb in the family and made the anemones very happy. Sapphire was lovingly massaging the creatures with her swordfish spade.

"Nice of you to join me. Usually, it's pulling tentacles to get you to do any work!"

Bowrain made a face at his big sister. "Okay," said Rainbow, "don't rub it in."

"Please start untangling the seaweed, Rainbow.

Bowrain, I need you to scrape barnacles off some of those beds and move them to the other side of the garden. Got that?"

With a sigh, Rainbow reached down and began to untangle and trim the seaweed. Bowrain took the sharp part of his fin and used it to pry up the barnacles.

"I'd do it again," said Bowrain.

"What about asking mom next time?" Rainbow suggested.

"She'll just say no," said Bowrain, heaving up a mass of creatures who fell away.

"Maybe not," said Rainbow, using the sharp end of her trident to untie a Gordian Knot of seaweed. "Let's look in on the savannah twins. No harm in that."

Bowrain nodded. "If we ask."

Beautiful Sapphire tied back a length of her blue black hair to keep it out of a bed of sick anemones. Gently, she scooped them into a living basket to treat in her clinic in a schooner hull. There was also a coral reef in need of refreshment. Some creatures had died, toxic from man-made chemicals. She had to remove them so the living could build anew.

Sapphire raised her trident above the sick part of the reef. An undercurrent flowed from it. Soon the whole area was bright and active, the dead washed down to deepest ocean. Rainbow wondered if she'd have the patience of her sister when she was older. Bowrain asked, "Where do you want these barnacles, lady?"

By dinner time the job was done. Sapphire, tired, leaned against the hull. "Thanks. You two did good work. Can I give you something?"

Bowrain said, "No. We didn't do this because we wanted to."

"But you did well, anyway. That deserves a prize."

"I deserve a prize any time!" laughed

Rainbow.

Sapphire went to the loveliest part of the anemone beds and removed one precious royal blue anemone and one of deepest hot pink. Rainbow chose the blue one and Bow-rain the pink.

"Do you have the covers?"

"Sorry!" said Sapphire, "I almost forgot." And from her hull, she removed two globes of clear plastic. "You know I scavenged these from those divers. They had trapped some coral creatures but dropped them when they saw me. I set the coral free. They love our castle."

Bowrain put the pink anemone in the globe and Sapphire did the same with the blue one. The globes filled with water and they latched them tight.

Rainbow said, "Thanks. I know you don't have many."

"They are special and rare and so are you two, don't forget it!" said Sapphire. Then she turned her back to clean her tools, before going to the hull.

The twins swam home to the Coral Castle. They paused in the hall between the bedrooms and then, in silent agreement, tip-finned across the hall.

Coast clear, thought Bowrain, though Rainbow was already in Glendora's room. Excitedly, she put the silver basin on the floor.

"Now!"

"One, two, three!!!"

The mertwins hurled the globes into the basin and jumped back from the pull, as the globes bobbed merrily down a whirlpool and into the hands of two startled twins of the Savannah. Bowrain and Rainbow looked into the basin and saw the twins standing knee-deep in lushly green irrigated savannah grass. Inside the globes, anemones floated in the same sea water that filled Glendora's magic basin.

CHAPTER 2

Of Bad Caves and Good, the Onyx Family begins Exploration.

Neptune called the family into his conference room. Around the octagonal onyx table were Sapphire, Emerald, baby Ruby, Bowrain, Rainbow, and Little Pinky on her clam shell.

Glendora swept into the sea green room, gorgeous in her electric eel mer gown. Neptune entered, fierce and solemn. He placed his Trident in a wall sconce and instantly warm light flooded the room. A benevolent smile lit his face as he greeted his assembled family with affectionate words for each child. Then Neptune unfurled an ancient map made of pressed water reeds. On it was drawn a U-shaped cove, with the Coral Castle at the center. Around it were a group of twelve caves. Some bore a red "X" at their entrances, while others had specific motifs, such as a unicorn or a bolt of lightning.

Rainbow felt very excited and sensed Bowrain's feelings matched her own. Unofficially, the always curious Mertwins were already exploring caves. Once they rescued Ruby, who launched her giggling self into a very fast current and ended up at a bad cave. Another expedition led to the discovery of Pinky, the mini mermaid Glendora had adopted at first sight. And then there were scrapes they were lucky to get out of alive. Of course their parents knew nothing of them and the twins wanted to keep it that way. Glendora still thought they were babies and Neptune wanted to control everything. But maybe someday it would be okay to tell their adventures. Rainbow's fin touched Bowrain's. It vibrated back. She thought, it's nice to have a twin who understands what you didn't say.

Neptune moved to the center of the table so all could follow his trident-shaped pointer. "Of these twelve caves, less than half have been explored. We have marked dangerous ones with an X. These are sealed with enchantments to protect unwary merfolk. The rest can be explored."

Neptune looked pointedly at Bowrain and Rainbow. His eyebrows knit over his flashing eyes. "You are to stay away from the sealed ones. Understand, your disobedience is not excused, but" and here his gaze betrayed amusement, "I am proud you have not needed my help. You have also provided valuable information so you are escaping punishment—for the moment. Don't do it again!" he thundered.

Rainbow and Bowrain flushed red orange hues from their pale pink skin to scarlet tails. Their father's "valuable" grandly reverberated in both their heads.

"I expect a full report on your caves! I trust that's clear? I have much work to do!" The green roof of the conference room immediately changed to sky.

Neptune raised one hand and caught a lightning bolt. With the other, he grabbed a rain cloud, and sailed high into the sky.

In truth, thought Rainbow, Father had more important things to do than rescue her and Bowrain. They used to pretend otherwise—how could he be busy all the time? They had done as they pleased, assuming Neptune would only let them go so far. Besides, Glendora kept track of their whereabouts in her basin. Today marked a new beginning. They must not let father down.

Neptune rested a moment from his exertions, beaming down from his vantage point in the heavens.

"Our cove should be a haven not just for Merfolk but anyone whose quest is pure knowledge. We need humans to participate."

There was a collective groan from the table. All knew how intractable humans could be in their gluttony for fish and searching for the wealth of black liquid underneath Neptune's sea. Rainbow was not paying attention. Her father's lectures always sounded dramatic and alarming. There was always some cause that caught his attention. Each time it was something of vital importance to the Earth and the seas, until he lost interest. Besides, even he knew the problems of allowing humans to be close to Merfolk. What was he thinking?

Instead, she thought of Boy Boy, her brown seahorse, and how she admired his bright vanilla colored polka dots.

Give me a break, dad, thought Bowrain, I know your job is important! But working with humans?

Just keep caves safe for humans, Glendora's thought went to Bowrain. After all, we share the planet with them.

Annoyed, she looked sternly at the twins, commanding

their attention. The problem with being Mer, they thought, was that you had no privacy. Everyone knew what someone else was thinking. You had only to tune in and listen. Glendora and Neptune exchanged a glance of flame. Then she smiled at Emerald, her eldest, born seconds before her sister, Sapphire, and perhaps Glendora's favorite, though she didn't acknowledge that idea.

Emerald, always quick to intuit her mother's purpose, generously stretched out her arms with a hug to welcome her siblings, Bowrain and Rainbow, into their newly responsible phase of life.

With her long flowing green hair and deep jewel-like eyes, Emerald was perhaps the loveliest Onyx with Sapphire an arguable second.

Though Emerald was the most like their mother in her thoughtful personality, Sapphire had Glendora's independent streak without the fury of young Rainbow. Her sharp critique of Neptune's plan echoed Glendora's own thoughts about the idiocy of including humans and the observation that he would get over this. Ideas broke over Neptune, fierce as the storms he created, and soon dissipated. Sapphire would protect the cove from intruders and watch her siblings.

Keeps her own council, thought Glendora. Wish I were so wise, thought Rainbow at the same moment. She gave a sigh, there was no privacy in her family.

"Twins," began Emerald, out loud at the conference table. "You're almost 1200, old enough to contribute to our family. Rainbow, don't roll your eyes! I don't mean like my job, minding Ruby and Pinky, though that's not hard for me. And Sapphire has the iridescent thumb in our family. We all love her garden. You two are natural explorers. That's why Dad gave you a mission. Take it seriously! With grown up tasks comes respect. You will earn yours."

Now Rainbow rolled her eyes.

"If you are rash and unthinking, don't count on a rescue. Take precautions. And think before you act."

"Safety first," said Glendora. "Take no chances."

"Be accurate in your reports," said Emerald. "Don't exaggerate to sound better. And it's time you learned to manage your thoughts. I'll show you how to shut out unwanted listeners and attract inspiration, surfing mind waves from outside sources without being identified."

"Your maps," said Neptune, sailing copies of the map of the cove to Bowrain and Rainbow. "I must distribute a cold front from Canada," he said and was gone.

"You two have curiosity and cleverness enough for this mission. You'll find the wisdom to see it through," said Glendora.

The twins felt her encouraging kiss. Eagerly they inspected their maps.

"Which caves, what will we need?" asked the twins. They saw a glowing white light on the map. It came from the last cave on the far right of the cove.

"Rainbow," Bowrain began excitedly.

"What took you so long?" she met his thought.

They looked up from their maps and realized they were

alone in the conference room. Emerald's voice reverberated in their heads. "This is your quest. None of us will tell you what to do."

"After you make your clam beds," finished Glendora. "Oh, no," groaned the twins.

Emerald laughed.. "You still have Mer school!"

"What do we need with that?" asked Bowrain. "We have work to do!"

"Knowledge or ignorance?"

Always right thought the twins, greatly annoyed. Emerald was their sister not their mother though she didn't seem to remember. The twins rolled their pliant map made of water reeds and swam back to their room. They picked up a shell of their favorite rock group, found lobster blasters and turned the sound up. "Crustaceans forever and ever" went the lyrics. It was the weekend. So there!

Emerald hated that group Rainbow thought, as her sister swam by, ears covered. Stories past yet now begun, thought Emerald. She bathed her spirit in a stream of tales about her beloved family. Past, present and future rolled over her like ocean waters always the same and always completely different.

CHAPTER 3

Ruby Goes to Sea and Ends Up in a Bad Cave

It was just before dawn in the Coral Castle. Baby Ruby stretched in her rocking clam and thought, "No one is up but me!" She stroked out of her shell and did a water somersault. She flipped her orangey red tail and kicked her purplish fins, delighted with the whirlpool she'd made. Happily she swam out of her castle room thinking, "I can move! And float." Ruby tickled a passing jellyfish and pulled the tentacle of a baby octopus. Its momma got huffy until she recognized Neptune's baby daughter. Then she let her baby wrap around Ruby and the two had a tug of war, pulling and letting go.

They fell into each other, laughing. Ruby floated with her new friend on the fast current. Then mom wrapped a tentacle around the baby and pulled it into more placid waters. Ruby went past, waving her fin not caring where she went. Ruby was having fun. She was only 350 years old.

Fun was not on Emerald Onyx's mind, when she rose at the sound of Ruby's giggle and saw her baby sister launch herself into a fierce current. Going somewhere fast, thought Emerald, as she stroked and paddled, keeping Ruby's red tail in sight. Soon she could see her silky light green baby hair, hear her excited gurgles, as she rolled over and over in the water's current.

"Ruby Onyx! Wait," Emerald called, hoping she'd move out of the current. But Ruby jackknifed herself further away in the swift current. Emerald dived into the current and flowed fast to her. Ruby laughed and waved, now further away. She thinks it's a game, Emerald worried. Must keep her in sight but where was she?

The current poured into a small cove. When Emerald reached it, Ruby was paddling her way into an adjacent cave. "Ruby!" She yelled and got an echoing giggle in reply.

Babies are so irritating, thought Emerald, who tied back her dark green hair with a cord made of a stretched squid tentacle threaded between two shells. There was no question that she would go after her despite the silvery X at the cave's entrance. The sign, which resembled embedded mica or sea foam, was unmistakable to sea creatures. This cave was off limits, an unknown fact to oblivious Ruby.

Maybe Dad used a repellant with a foul smell? There was also a hissing sound, probably more stimulant than deterrent to a creature as curious as Ruby Onyx.

Cautiously, Emerald followed her nose into the cave, assured by the acrid air, bubbles and hisses of a hot spring inside. Judging by the temperature, who knew she wouldn't find a boiled baby mermaid there also? The hot water was cloudy, with a yucky, greasy feeling but in she went.

Then she heard a piercing "Emerald!"

From nowhere came a shot of flame. Emerald dived

underwater and probed with mermaid sight. At the bottom of the steamy pool was a mountain of glittering metal. Emerald grabbed what she thought was an encrusted barnacle but it was no creature. The coating rubbed off to reveal a jewel the size of an egg. At that moment the glittering mountain moved.

She heard a roar and Ruby's scream.

Emerald broke the surface of the water in the cave. Through the steam, opposite her dark green head, were the huge yellow headlight eyes of a dark scaly dragon. Emerald held the jewel between her thumb and forefinger.

"Put that back!" the dragon roared, shooting flame. The hiss was behind her dive. She stayed down. He whined piteously, "Come back, please. I won't hurt you. Don't drop the diamond!"

Emerald broke through the water's surface and was surrounded by steam. The dragon's gaze did not falter from the stone. His words were courtly and careful.

"My name is Clyde. Welcome to my cavern." "Where is my sister?"

"That is bad manners. First tell me your name."

"Hiding babies is appalling manners."

"Impertinent fish!" he lashed out his tail but she dove below the hard stinger to the mucky bottom. Emerald found two rocks and hoped they were gems. She cleaned them off. One was a sapphire of deep blue, the other a ruby so big it filled her hand. She surfaced to hot turmoil. Waves stirred in the foul mist of dragon breath.

"Robber!" Clyde roared indignantly.

"Give back my sister."

The dragon sprayed steamy water on his paw. It cleaned off a layer of brown muck. There, revealed, was a small dehydrated Ruby Onyx. She shrieked, "Emerallll!" Emerald's heart flipped. A fountain of cold clean water streamed from the still tiny trident around her neck.

A potent charm, the trident changed size and function as needed to protect a child of Neptune. Ruby revived and began to whimper. Emerald thought to Ruby, "Go to sleep. You're okay now."

"Mamma?" Ruby thought back.

"You'll see her soon." And, in her mind, Emerald crooned a lullaby to tired Ruby. With her happy baby smile Ruby soon fell asleep, her red tail delicate as a feather in the dragon's paw.

"So tender. I am looking forward to her," said Clyde longingly.

"Aren't water dragons vegetarians?" "Some of us like fish."

"I like jewels."

"Mermaids adorn their beauty with live jewels like sea anemones."

"Mineral jewels spruce up coral reefs and look great in a garden."

"Have we come to an impasse fair mermaid?"

"I want my sister back. You want your jewels. How do we proceed?"

Clyde's headlight eyes dimmed thoughtfully. "What

about a simultaneous handover?"

"We are in your cavern," Emerald pointed out his advantage.

"True, true," said Clyde, and a hot geyser erupted under Emerald sending her, flailing to the ceiling of the cavern. Below was the fiery open mouth of the dragon. "And you might be nice, steamed...."

"I thought dragons were known for their hospitality," said Emerald, angrily. She watched Ruby turn fitfully in her sleep on the rough paw. "If I wasn't Neptune's daughter and I didn't know my father was looking for us, I'd be nervous."

The dragon met Emerald's gaze, fierce as her father's. "And you're not?" he asked, languidly stretching his torso. Amid clinking sounds, his scales changed from green to gold to black.

"Nervous for you, when he catches up with us," she said. Instantly, the geyser disappeared hurling Emerald back into the cavern's hot pool. She quickly surfaced. "When Neptune explored this cave, didn't he allow you to stay on certain conditions?"

"Truth is, I don't even like fish," said Clyde. "In fact, I don't need food. Haven't touched it for a few thousand years."

"What do you live on?"

"Minerals and memories. I have total recall"

Considerately Clyde placed Ruby on a flat rock. He scooped up muddy soil and poured it into his mouth. After a few minutes, he shot the mud out of his mouth and crunched on something with great satisfaction. "Love that rock, lots of copper. I like all minerals, though never touch gold. Too soft but perfect to sleep on for a few hundred years."

"What do you want from a mermaid?"

"Conversation. You know it's been eons since I've had a companion as charming as you."

"Lovely compliment," said Emerald, hoisting herself out of the water on a rock in sight of Ruby. She stretched out the length of her steamy green gold azure tail and flapped her fins, sticky with mineral vapor.

"You need no adornment."

"Jewels would be shamed by my beauty?"

"I want my sister back. You want your jewels. How do we proceed?"

"As a matter of fact, yes," said Clyde, lowering his lashes over his eyes—planets of liquid amber fringed by shadow.

"And dragons know the best stories."

"You mermaids are famous for song. May I have one?" "It's a trade?"

"A song for a story."

Emerald looked at him and Clyde's black scales blushed purplish.

"My sister for a song?"

"And my jewels. To show my good faith, I'll give you your sister."

Clyde lifted the rock which held the slumbering Ruby and dropped her into Emerald's arms. Emerald sang in Dolphin calls and seagull language which followed her mermaid sight to Glendora's sitting room. Her mother was also singing, as she arranged cuttings from Sapphire's garden in her silver basin.

Emerald looked into her mother's basin and was transported visually to Sapphire's beautiful garden. She sang of her love for the creatures of many colors and textures. Emerald's song brought Sapphire's refreshing garden into the fetid cavern. When Clyde's eyelids descended like velvet curtains, Emerald, carefully holding Ruby, slipped back into the pool.

A giant claw barred her way. A large eyelid lifted to show an even bigger glaring yellow eye ball. "Jewels?" Clyde hissed.

Emerald rolled over. From underneath her tail fin, she

picked out encrusted white diamonds, rubies, and emeralds. Clyde grabbed them with pleasure. Lazily, he let each one slide over his head and rest on his back. With a hugely satisfied smile, he ordered, "Sing some more!"

Emerald did not resist. When did she have a more appreciative audience than this sad dragon? She sang of Ruby and Glendora. How Glendora united her spirit with the sea, the cradle of all life, and calmed her baby, with its ever moving unchanging song. She sang of Boy Boy and Guy Guy, the reverse colored polka dot seahorses stabled below the castle. One was yellow with brown dots, the other chocolate brown with banana dots; friends and rivals infinitely faithful to the Onyx family.

She sang of Rainbow and Bowrain, racing the seahorses after merschool, before their steeds brought them to the Coral Castle for homework. She sang of Neptune's powerful square back, his muscles straining as he pulled down clouds and hurled storms at continents. She sang herself into the pool and swam towards the front of the cave, holding Ruby close to her chest. Clyde stirred himself and she halted, her distrust of the dragon returning.

"Whom do I have the pleasure of listening to?" he asked.

"Emerald Onyx, eldest daughter of Neptune and Glendora."

"Honored. I hope you will not give a bad a report of me," he purred, if a harsh fiery throat could do such a thing.

She felt a hard object thud against her rear scales and investigated with her free hand. The emerald hard in her hand was an electric green.

"Your name-stone, princess of the deep. With it goes my promise of welcome if ever you're pleased to visit."

"Another day!" Emerald sang out sweetly and, with Ruby securely under her arm, she splashed herself out of the cave. Ruby woke up, crying. Emerald hushed her, as she located a swiftly moving current.

"Ruby, we're going home." "Mamma!" she said enthusiastically.

"Yes. Suppose I wasn't here to rescue you?"

Ruby whimpered and curled up tighter against Emerald, twirling her dark green hair in her fingers, tugging a little and laughing.

"Cut it out, Ruby!" Emerald said, also laughing.

She hugged her baby sister, tears spilling from her happy eyes. Just suppose I wasn't here, she thought, glad Ruby was all right.

"You mustn't go out all alone until you're big. Understand?"

Ruby was solemn a moment, "Ruby unnerstand…"

"Now Mommy!" She yelled gleefully, her tail enthusiastically flapping in the current, the fin jabbing Emerald's side.

"Ruby, relax!"

To that end, Emerald sang about the Coral Castle and the comfortable shell bed her sister had been in only that morning. Home, where with luck, Emerald would find Glendora. Wasn't it her time to take charge?

HER *idea began deep under water, where she saw a piece of torn cloth fluttering under a funny set of metal chains with great cylinders attached.*

CHAPTER 4

Sapphire's 16th birthday at the Coney Island Mermaid Parade

Sapphire Onyx was turning 1600 in Mer years, 16 as humans tell time, and all the creatures under the sea were preparing presents for the beloved daughter of King Neptune. But this year she also planned her own personal celebration.

Her idea began deep under water, where she saw a piece of torn cloth fluttering under a funny set of metal chains with great cylinders attached. On the cloth was a portrait of a proud mermaid. It was obviously from the surface, yet Sapphire wondered; could mermaids live on land? If they were like the portrait, she wanted to meet them and perhaps know something her father didn't. Above the mermaid on the cloth was the word "Parade" and a date, June 21st, as they kept days on the surface.

Near June 4, my birthday, Sapphire thought and corrected herself. *Our birthday!* Emerald, was born on the same date, just a few seconds before. Was it that tiny fact that made her act superior? Sapphire hugged her plan close to her consciousness. No matter how Emerald probed, *what was her twin's secret,* she learned nothing. Sapphire distracted her with new anemone decorations for her tail,

ALMOST a different species, she thought, zooming in on two mermaids with orange and yellow hair cut in a flat straight line

or pink eel extensions for her hair. Anything to misdirect her sister's piercing thought waves from Coney Island. And today was *her day.*

Shyly, Sapphire poked her head up from the sea and looked at the sky. Now that she was of age she could break the surface, though she had to consider the ancient warning about showing herself.

Yet what harm could there be in wanting to see land-based mermaids—kin? She would wait and they would swim by.

Sapphire imagined a parade, Mer folk swimming in a line with much noise and laughter. She would join the singing, as they went from one part of the island to the other.

She found a good rock not too close to the boardwalk, though close enough to see it and the waters that must bring her folk. Sapphire took out her abalone mirror and comb of shark's teeth. Neptune said whole eternities passed in the time it took his daughters to comb their hair. Patience was a mermaid trait.

Sapphire's long hair was blue black and turquoise. As she brushed, it shone like sea foam touched with sky. In the mirror, she looked to the water but on the boardwalk saw a strange assembly of sea creatures. *Almost a different species*, she thought, zooming in on two mermaids with orange and yellow hair cut in a flat straight line, holding a banner. The long purplish hair of another mermaid was filled with sea creatures of an unfathomable shiny material.

They could not be living things, she thought. *And what is that fearsome creature?* More demon than Mer, it bared fangs at several men holding black boxes at funny angles. Suns popped from the boxes and faded. Then Sapphire noticed, floating in the demon mermaid's forehead, a curious eyeball. *Unseeing*, she thought, *in an unreal eye socket, like the rest of the creature. Were there no natural sights?*

She spotted a young boy with green streaky skin and dull whitish hair carrying a red trident of some inert material. His face looked happy and stunned. *Perhaps overwhelmed with people looking at him. Taking his image?* His feet were covered by wisps of colored fabric. Behind him, a maternal looking woman wore a dress of a slithery texture. A closer look showed a bright coral reef pictured in the fabric. She called encouragement to the boy and smiled.

A mother? They were natural but totally foreign, Sapphire thought with disappointment. What had any of these people to do with Earth mermaids? Fascinated by the humans, she replaced her mirror and comb between scales. Pulling her tail out from under her, she prepared for a grand arc from her rock on the shore to the water. At that moment, a sun popped and she was looking at a short man with a green beard and a kind of nonseaweed skirt around his round belly yelling, "Gotcha!"

He had round black glass spheres over his eyes which made her uncomfortable, since he could see into her eyes but she could not glimpse his. He looked at her as though she were something good to eat.

"Wow, a spectacular costume."

"It's just me," Sapphire said, embarrassed.

"Like a fish out of water. I'm Roger, photographer with the Astoria Press. I was told there was a number with a mermaid diving into the water. It's supposed to be at the end of the parade and there's a band playing. Where's your band?"

Sapphire looked around her wondering, what band? There was Neptune's orchestra, but they could not rise to the surface. She concentrated a moment, conjured a large conch shell from the water, and handed it to the little man. He was astonished, more so when she gestured he should hold it to his ear. And what a full brass sound filled his ears! He put the shell down, then held it up in disbelief and finally, handed it back to Sapphire. "Don't know how you did that. Where's it coming from? That's not a band, we're talking about an orchestra.

"Can you do that again?" he asked, taking out his

camera. "I never saw a blushing mermaid before." At that moment he shot her with his camera. She felt like hiding. More of the blush colored her skin, to the man's further delight. And just when she felt he was a true pest to be sent on his way, he turned to a cacophony of sound.

There, running toward her on the beach, amid shining instruments, trumpets and trombones, flutes and drums at full shriek, was a motley group of players carrying a long white cloth. Lots of feeling, but quite lacking in skill, she thought. They were unable to make melodies. But dissonance has it uses, she thought, balancing her love of harmonies with its opposite. *Perhaps they need my help to balance?*

As the group got closer, Sapphire emitted a peal of sound unlike anything the rushing crowed had heard. They stopped and shrieked, "That's good! Amazing!" Two men with grayish skin and funny yellow straw around their waists flourished their torn banner. MERMAID PARADE! Then she heard the giggling voice behind them. It belonged to the mergirl she had seen on the cloth at the bottom of the sea. At last, Sapphire thought. She was off the rock, her arms around the mermaid, and they both fell in the sand.

"Well, really. I like you too but isn't this taking it too

Far?"

Sapphire tried to understand what she meant. Far but they were near?

"I've so wanted to meet an earth mermaid," she burbled in the eerie toots and gurgly sounds of her own language. But the mergirl just looked perplexed. Then Sapphire got it.

She smelled it, the acrid sweat. Human smell combined with sickly sweet make-up running down the girl's cheeks. Her yellow hair had wispy dark hair underneath and it didn't move like any hair Sapphire'd ever seen. Then the mergirl got up and walked on two legs. She looked at Sapphire with annoyance and amusement. "How do you navigate that?" she asked, pointing to Sapphire's tail.

Sapphire arranged herself, so it seemed like she was just relaxing on the sand, not beached. Meanwhile, the photographer from the Astoria Press placed the banner near her and aimed his black box at it, while the rest of the raucous group sipped turquoise cold drinks with pretty parasols in them. The earth mergirl whispered about Sapphire and they were suddenly very quiet.

One of the men with the straw skirts understood. "I've had a lot to drink, but there's something different about you." The girl looked at Sapphire. "Are you a real mermaid?"

Sapphire smiled and then hurled her body upward from the beach over the water, a huge curving arc into the air. Scales and tail and white flesh hovered for a moment, her dark hair statically alive in the air.

She looked to earth at the small group on the beach. As one being they yelled, "Don't go!" The photographer's lens leaped to catch her flight. In that moment, Sapphire made her decision. She fell in a straight line as if from the sky into the ocean. "AHHH!" said the humans who, she realized, wanted to be mermaids. In an instant, she soared to the surface, arms overhead a little distance from the group.

"Will you join us?" asked the photographer. "You will

make my photos famous!"

"Will you join us," said the girl, "I have always wanted to meet a real mermaid!"

"Please come back," said the two straw-garbed men who appeared as twins. One said, "I have never seen anyone as beautiful as you."

"Please play your music," pleaded the musicians. And then the little boy, still covered in streaky green make-up, met her eyes at the edge of the ocean. "What is your name? Will you play with me?"

"Sure. I'm celebrating my birthday."

"How old are you," asked the boy, all inquisitive. "Sixteen hundred, 16 in human years," said the Mermaid, "and that's pretty old when you think it's a hundred for every one of your earth years." While she spoke, Sapphire swam swiftly to the shallow waves where the boy waited. The others ran to meet her, their band's cacophony drowned out by Sapphire's strange voice. Strangely, the identical sound came from the opposite end of the beach!

If it wasn't Emerald Onyx, her own annoying sister!

Emerald stuck out her pointed tongue, "It's my birthday too!"

Sapphire and Emerald exchanged a mermaid thought. Humans were unpredictable and acquisitive about sea creatures. While the mermaids hadn't listened to the ancient edict about not showing themselves, they weren't fools. Together they sang an enchantment that inspired wondrous thoughts of fellowship and fun. Buried in the humans were ideas about nets and coast guard calls, capture and fortunes to be made. And so the twins and the Earthly Mer people played in the ocean, waved the banner, until it got too soggy, and posed for photos.

Sapphire offered the photographer a ride. He held her around the waist, resting on her huge tail—hanging on for dear life in the rough waves. Little did he care about his camera, which disappeared.

The young earth boy, who wanted to be Mer, asked, "Can I be next?" She looked into his clear hazel eyes. "Gladly," she answered, "but we will have to come back."

He said, "I know. But seeing you is very special. For years, people have said you do not exist, that I have too much imagination. You are a wish come true."

Sapphire stroked his wild-looking white hair. White paint came off on her hand.

"Sorry," he said apologetically. "My hair's really brown."

"I have always wanted to know a merboy like you." Mutely, his eyes beseeched her.

"Yes. You are of Earth and the sea!"

And the boy, destined to be a marine biologist, rode the Mermaid to the bottom of the ocean, breathing as she did.

Then, they swam back to the Coney Island Beach where his mother anxiously awaited him.

"Now go," said Sapphire. "Who knows that we won't meet in another hundred years?" The boy smiled with wonder and put his arms around Sapphire. She kissed his forehead.

"What's your name?" "Charlie."

"Charlie, you have been kissed by a real mermaid."

And Sapphire swam off, Emerald following. They were synchronized in their own field of movement, oblivious to the beach party. Lots of Earth Merfolk were swaying and drinking turquoise drinks, showing off their outfits, and splashing each other in the water. There were lots of shrieks as wet sequin tails sunk in the wavelets. Off-key trombone sounds carried in the wind. Charlie looked after her, the light in his eyes reflecting in the dark water.

His mother gathered him in a beach towel with the image of a long mermaid upon it. Charlie wrapped the terry cloth tail around him and gazed upon the water. His mother sat on a step down from the boardwalk.

"I'm tired," she said. "It's been a long parade."

The boy looked at her differently now. Her costume made of plastic sheeting printed with a coral reef wasn't the same to him. "Mom, some guy said you look like a walking shower curtain."

"And aren't you the savage to repeat it." She touched his forehead. "Is that a tattoo?"

"What do you mean?"

"Looks like a tiny tattoo shell there, where your hair starts."

"Nothing, mom," said Charlie. He rubbed the spot. It felt scaly.

CHAPTER 5

Rainbow seeks adventure and finds Pinky Onyx

Rainbow Onyx was sick of her brother always thinking he knew best, just because he was a boy! Bowrain even assumed he was Neptune's heir, though there had been MerQueens in the Onyx family! Who was he to tell her she couldn't go off without him, that she needed him to protect her? Hadn't she been the one to rescue him from Mamma's silver basin? And it wasn't the first time. He thought he should be in charge, but actually she was born first and, like most girls, had more sense.

Bowrain was asleep in his bed cave, softly lit by phosphorescent fish and plants, when she swam past, muffling the water motion with her cozy fin socks.

The room was too light for her because, though he wouldn't admit it, Bowrain was afraid of the dark.

With Bowrain safely adrift in dream land, Rainbow excitedly swam back for her supplies. She would prove herself a worthy successor to the Trident throne. From the central curl of the pink shell, she took Neptune's map of unexplored caves, folded to a tidy square. She placed it in her supply girdle with a flask of eel oil for tight places, dried seaweed salad with mervitamins, a detangling comb, starfish compass, and a recording conch for her observations. Then Rainbow tied her long greenish blonde hair back with a glowing flexi worm. Time to make some speed.

There was a math quiz at Merschool tomorrow, and Neptune and Glendora would not be pleased if she scored poorly, having been out half the night.

She already knew her sand tables but could use the drill. One bucket of sand held a hundred mer trillion grains, two buckets were two hundred mer trillion, she reviewed while swimming down the corridors of the Coral Castle, past Bowrain and her sleeping sisters, Emerald and Sapphire.

She paused at Ruby's giggles and peered in to see the baby mermaid tickling herself in a silly dream in her rocking shell. Ruby was such a dear when she was sleeping. At her parents' door, Rainbow swam faster and closer to the opposite corridor. Glendora's ability to monitor her children, even in deep sleep, was well known. And Neptune was highly keyed to irregularities in the atmosphere. But if they felt her pass by their room, it was momentary and there was no pursuit.

Then she was in the stable with her own seahorse!

Instantly awake, Boy Boy nuzzled her shoulder and bobbed up and down.

Against his chocolate brown skin the banana yellow polka dots were a blur of excitement. Unmistakably also looking for action was Guy Guy, Bowrain's mount. Rainbow patted his velvety yellow muzzle and the brown dots on his mane. "Bowrain will come later," she whispered. Guy Guy's eyes were sparkly at the thought of his beloved master.

Rainbow let Boy Boy out and relatched the paddock.

He stretched out his curling bottom and eagerly licked Rainbow's face. She gave him a nugget of sea salt and gently pulled herself side saddle onto his sleek brown hair. Soon his yellow dots glowed palely in the moonlight, matching the color of her hair whipping behind her. They kept a mad pace, skimming across the surface of the water, angled so the current helped them keep their course.

Soon they had left the coral castle behind and were fast approaching the unexplored cave. Without warning, a large water funnel arose around them. A huge geyser blew up under them, and Rainbow and Boy Boy no longer had control or direction. In the dizzying ascent high over the ocean, she saw in the distance a fiery flame engulfing a cave, and Neptune's silvery trident baring the entrance reinforcing the "X."

It was a fearsome sight. Rainbow clung to her seahorse, while Boy Boy curled himself around her, so they would not be separated. Then she got used to riding high on a moving mountain of water. She and her seahorse were one stable entity.

"Boy Boy, don't move!" Taking her map from her girdle, she confirmed their destination, the fiery cave.

Rainbow spoke into her conch shell, recording, "Seahorse and Mermaid mission begun. We easily spotted the unexplored cave and no wonder, it's covered with flame and guarded by geysers. More, later!"

Rainbow took her tiny trident charm from her neck and shot a thin flame from the top of the water mountain to

THEY *found themselves looking up at a giant chubby face with bright curious blue eyes and a soft red mouth.*

the X on the distant cave wall. A thin bridge formed and the water flowed over it, allowing Rainbow and Boy Boy to follow.

Rainbow again took out her recording conch. "The cave is covered with fire as Boy Boy and I carefully approach."

"Now what?" she asked Boy Boy. "Do we go in?"

Boy Boy's fear showed in the yellows of his eyes. He was about to turn tail, when a ball of fire, followed by a ball of water, knocked him down. Rainbow was gasping from being scorched and soaked, when a large chubby hand shot out of the cave and pulled her and Boy Boy inside.

They found themselves looking up at a giant chubby

face with bright curious blue eyes and a soft red mouth. A forest of dark curls filled the head. I could get lost there, Rainbow thought, or worse....don't put me in that mouth!

But the creature laughed at her horrified expression and shook her up and down in its fist, squealing. He had Boy Boy in the other hand and began clunking them together.

"Getting the life squeezed out of me!" Boy Boy neighed to the immense delight of the monster. He squeezed again, and Boy Boy neighed. Brother, thought Rainbow, the creature thinks we're toys.

"Don't neigh!" she shouted to Boy Boy and sure enough, the next time he was squeezed, Boy Boy didn't react, though his red head was almost bursting.

The creature's brow furrowed with frustration. He hurled Boy Boy down, where luckily he landed on one of the many geysers that filled the bottom of the cave. Then the fickle creature turned to Rainbow and held her upside down, flapped her tail with his finger and, when she screamed, put her right side up and held her by her hair. Rainbow screamed again and the big finger went close to her face. She bit with her sharp teeth. Then she was down on the Geyser but the earth was trembling with the wails of the creature.

From her height at the top of a geyser, she could see the immense size of the wailing creature. Like a human baby but huge, she thought. His body was as fat and round as his face. His open crying mouth had no teeth but soft red gums. Fearsome, Rainbow thought. A moment before he grabbed at her tail, she grabbed a scale flask of oil of eel.

Slippery work to catch her, though his tears were instantly dry and his squeals became laughs, as he clutched at the mermaid. Then something hit him in the eye and he was on the soft white cloth of his rear end, again wailing.

Rainbow looked down and saw her seahorse readying another rock in what looked like a slingshot. Her glow worm hair fastener! Greenish blonde hair was around her and she hadn't even noticed, so bent was she on avoiding those hands. And it was now her hair roughly held in those same huge baby hands. Rainbow felt a nasty tug, saw a piece of hair floating and thought, in a moment he's going to put me in his mouth. Babies always put everything in their....

Rainbow thought she was about to die, when a door off the dark cavern opened. Huge pounding as a form emerged; legs like skyscrapers, arms big as boulders and hands like airplanes that scooped up the giant baby.

He dropped Rainbow at once and she fell again into the turmoil of water. When she surfaced, she saw a familiar brown shape and draped her exhausted body over faithful Boy Boy. The giantess, like an experienced mother, soothed her baby. Rainbow and Boy Boy cowered in the cavern resounding with the baby's cries, before the giantess carried him back through an opening in the cavern, saying, "Tsk, tsk, now Bartholomew, I'll get you something to eat. She stopped, sniffing. "Maybe some meat or fish," and her eyes darted around the cave.

"Hold on," neighed Boy Boy, who dived with Rainbow away from the Giantess' perceptive nose.

The two swam underwater, until they felt the vibrations

of her steps out of the cave. Never was Rainbow so glad to see the open sky.

Rainbow rolled off Boy Boy and frolicked in the sunshine, surfing silvery waves. A free mermaid once more, she ran races with Boy Boy. Little did she think of going back to the Coral Castle, until her hair became tangled in a clear jellyfish. She heard a bell-like call, a tinkling voice. *Imagination or the wind?* Rainbow got her detangle comb from her girdle and began to detach the sticky jelly from her bedraggled hair. How she wished she still had her hair worm to pull the mess back. Again, the curious tinkling music. She stopped combing to listen for the location, amplified in the jellyfish.

She spied what she thought might be a mini-mermaid. *Perhaps one from the race of mini-mermaids, who lived in a distant ocean? So tiny,* thought Rainbow, who squinted closely at the jellyfish's translucent body.

There, in the center of the jelly fish, was a young mermaid the size of her pinky finger. She fed the jelly fish a small piece of her seaweed mervitamins. As its mouth opened, out swam the creature. Rainbow had never seen a mini mermaid before.

She opened her cupped palms. The pink haired mermaid called up to her in a tinkly voice, "Thanks for releasing me!"

Rainbow looked at Pinky with wonder at her every detail. Like herself, but so delicate she couldn't help staring. "Where do you come from?"

Pinky looked around her. "I'm not sure where it is from

here. Can I go with you?"

Rainbow smiled, "I am a daughter of Neptune. You can come with me to the Coral Castle."

"Sister!" Pinky said. "I have often heard of my father and so longed to see him."

Rainbow knew there was only one Neptune. It felt odd to think her father had another family; that she had a sister she didn't even know.

"My mother's name is Glendora. Would you like to meet her?"

Pinky nodded happily. Rainbow got on Boy Boy and placed Pinky safely in the indentation where her skin stopped and scales began. They made their way through the soft waves of that placid ocean.

The Queen of the mini-mermaids had long curly red brown hair, eyes of deep chartreuse and lips the soft pink inside a conch shell. At six inches, she was the average length for her race with an electric tail that alternated between blue and red.

Called Esmeralda Fish Eyes because she saw as fishes do, the Queen always felt currents before she even knew her own direction.

Often her clan was mistaken for glittering minnows and they were happy to mimic their friends because it lessened the chance of human discovery. Within memory, no mini-mermaid had been caught in mankind's nets and it was Esmeralda's responsibility to keep it so.

Yesterday morning she had tuned her brain to the deep caverns of the Pacific Rim, where her sisters, daughters and mothers lived in hive-like clusters. Not just commands and admonitions, but her smallest insights and trepidations were instantly communicated. Though as a child, she had had to learn to block communications less than useful to herself.

This morning, as she swam among the clusters of sleeping mini mermaids, she had taken a kind of inventory. There was her sister, Clotilde the Brunette, and her daughter, Arion, the stripe-haired.

They were part of the royal cluster, a dormitory which also included her own daughters Algaeon and Anemonia.

Both were resting in a scavenged porthole lined with soft sea sponges. They stirred, rolled over spoon style and continued to sleep, aware of her presence like a small ripple.

Esmeralda made her way to the baby minis, where dozens of very tiny mermaids were continually rocked in their shells. *Where was Rapture, her most maternal daughter, who tended the babies?* She could see Oh Boy, her faithful seahorse dozing above the shells with one eye open.

Immediately, he came to Esmeralda. "Where is Rapture?"

Oh Boy bobbed worriedly. The bright green polka dots in his fuchsia form became emerald. "Here a moment ago."

She didn't need her eyes to know that Rapture was not in the area. She didn't need to see her pink hair and yellowish tail with honey highlights to conjure up her missing daughter.

Where had she gone? Esmerelda knew her wayward daughter was tempted by tide pools on the other side of the world. She longed to see her father, Neptune Onyx. Unknowingly, he had drawn her away from the safety of her mother. She might have guessed.

Esmeralda was aware that such a time would come.

The pull to visit her father was powerful. She pictured Neptune and his other family and sensed for Rapture. She had not reached him. *That was a worry!* Esmeralda had loved Neptune Onyx, when he had fallen into their caverns, surprised and pleased by the existence of her delicate race.

They had enjoyed their time together but always knew it would end. Her kingdom was a matriarchy, as his was a patriarchy.

No males could stay and none were needed. Each mini mermaid was inseparable from the whole hive. Neptune posed disruption. He must found a separate family. So they had parted. But he had left her a gift, a pod of his own. And she loved this special merchild, who grew to resemble her father. She thought of him, when she admired Rapture's strong features, so different from the mobile quality of her own. She thought of the ebb and flow of Neptune's fierce crashing love. High winds and churning waves one instant, placid motion the next. He was the instant.

CHAPTER 6

Aunt Yoshiba reveals Onyx family history

Rainbow rolled over in her twin waterbed and her iridescent purple tail sloshed and flopped onto the floor. She opened her eyes, dove out of the aquarium window and swam to Neptune's stables, thinking of the comfort and company of a journey by sea horse. When she reached her sea horse Boy Boy, he was happily snoring. The yellow and brown polka dots on his flanks rippled to reverse, as the water moved through his gills. She crept close and whispered, "Let's explore a bad cave."

Immediately awake, Boy Boy whinnied, "I don't want to get into trouble! "

"Come on, it will be fun. Don't be such a seawuss!"

"And you, with the fiercest father of all oceans!"

"Aren't I the fiercest mergirl?" she flounced, her tail jutting outward to match her lower lip.

"You are truly a princess," said Boy Boy with an attitude not entirely lost on Rainbow.

Before she could reply, Guy Guy, the polka dot seahorse of chocolate hue with yellow dots, said, "I'm in."

Boy Boy said, "Don't go!"

FISHTAILS *together, heads close, mermaid and seahorse plowed through water on what was to become a glorious morning.*

"Don't sweat it. The big guy will know she talked me into it."

"Good bye then," said Rainbow, and they were off.

Fishtails together, heads close, mermaid and seahorse plowed through water on what was to become a glorious morning. As the water took sunlight, they made haste to put space and time before the moment of discovery—that she was gone.

Happily whooshing through a bed of protesting bivalves they spotted a green glow-in-the-dark pulsing circular form. Tentacles, they both observed, curiously hung, wreath-like at the entrance to a cave. Rainbow was excited.

"Let's see what's attached to this!"

"No way I'm going in there," said Guy Guy "Then stay!"

Rainbow flipped her fin at the seahorse, gone in an instant. Impulsive, Guy Guy grumbled, following. What a job it was to keep her in sight. He fell against her. Rainbow had halted, mesmerized by the owner of the tentacles, a giant glowing squid. Further inside the cave, they saw long flowing Mer hair framing a woman's beautiful but stern face. *Like a statue, her gaze inward,* Rainbow thought. With some difficulty she tore herself from the face to where fins should have been. Instead, squid tentacles curled in a pile. Without meeting Rainbow's eyes, the creature said, "I see you met my pet, Ashiba. I'm Yoshiba and I used to know your father."

"Was he your friend?"

"We are brother and sister. Our father was Zeus. My mother was a squid."

"Auntie! How come I never met you?"

"I've been away for some years at Squid Expo in Atlantis under the Sea. If you look closely at your father's tail, you'll see that he has a small tentacle less than an inch long. It's a birthmark."

Then Rainbow felt a large bottom tentacle wrap itself around her middle section in a tight hug. She felt a moment of panic, unable to escape. Any minute this new relative could become a foe. The tentacle loosened. He aunt's voice boomed. "Sorry if I scared you. It's how squid folk hug and hunt."

Rainbow wrapped her tail around the squid half, her upper body arms around Aunt Yoshika's neck, a heartfelt hug. "That's what merfolk do," she said.

At that moment, a whirlpool formed around them and Rainbow was sucked around and around. She came apart from her aunt landing on ocean bottom with flat curving coral and unmoving trees. One whirled around and, what she thought was a tree, was a Ninja squid. Tentacle layers, tightly wrapped like bandages around its body revealed only eyes. Whirling, long tentacles shot out and Guy Guy was wrapped and squeezed.

Rainbow removed her tiny trident from her neck. It expanded to the size of her hand. She hurled the trident and, rotating fast as a Ninja's star, it cut through the tentacles. Guy Guy neighed his thanks, as the creature bounded away.

Still, listening for she knew not what, Rainbow heard a series of giggles. She saw three prancing mermaids holding star fish spread like Japanese fans.

They had white faces with crimson red coral mouths, and long inky black Mer hair held up with driftwood chopsticks. In unison they sang, "We sea maids three, laugh and sing, back and forth in the foam." In chirps they repeated the refrain and Rainbow thought she had never seen such precious mermaids. At the end of the entertainment, Aunt Yoshiba smoothed her tentacles, and sat on a shiny seat of black abalone.

"Welcome to the Coral Palace of a Thousand Mermaids," said Yoshiba. "We Coral Mermaids and Ninja squids get along very well here. Would you stay awhile and get to know your aunt?"

"I am supposed to be in Mer School today," said Rainbow. I don't know that Dad's happy with me for leaving and not saying where I'm going. I was hoping to be back before they noticed. What's the best way to get back to the Coral Castle?"

Aunt Yoshiba frowned, "Such a short visit! Your father has not kept in touch. But then, neither have I. Come back some time and bring your brother. I will create a water tunnel for you to travel back to your home. "Come with me!"

Aunt Yoshiba swam some distance upward and began to spiral her body, rapidly turning over and over. Soon there was a tunnel of water in motion. Rainbow, riding Guy Guy, went into the fast moving water.

"Bye, Aunt Yoshiba!" she called. Flipping her fin and a bit dizzy, Rainbow arrived in the familiar waters above the Coral Castle. But she would soon return. There was much she wanted to ask her mysterious aunt.

When Rainbow and Guy Guy reached the stables, her father awaited them in a fierce temper.

"You have disobeyed me! There was Merschool today and you are not to go into unknown caves!" He roared, so angrily, Guy Guy thought he should share the blame.

"I was with her, sir," said Guy Guy. "She was determined but not without help."

"You leave Guy Guy unstabled, drifting on a post!" "Dad," said Rainbow. "Can I see your fin?"

"What are you talking about!" he roared, but not as loudly.

"You'll see," she smiled her most coaxing smile, "Don't be an old sour Neptune."

THEY *had white faces with crimson red coral mouths, and long inky black Mer hair held up with driftwood chopsticks.*

Her dad was never angry at her long. Playfully, she looked under his fin.

"That tickles," he laughed, as she looked for his tentacle and found it.

"Your birthmark. Aunt Yoshiba has the same!"

Neptune paused. "It was her you saw. I forgot about Yoshiba. Let's go see her, it's been a long time but we were always friends."

Rainbow was scarcely on Guy Guy's back, when her father called a huge whirlpool that hurled them to the cave.

"The sea shuttle!" said Neptune proudly.

They dived to the depths of the cave and came up. "We probably have to go underneath Yoshiba's caves to catch her," began Neptune, examining the length of the cave. Rainbow and Guy Guy traveled the circumference with eel light. But there was no iridescence, no Yoshiba.

Neptune took note of Rainbow's sad face. "Now don't hold it against your aunt. Like all Atlantians, she's here one minute, gone the next. It's not that we don't care about those we love, we just want to keep swimming. She'll be in touch. You've made contact. Check your eel-mail."

Rainbow felt a tear. Sometimes it seemed so many creatures came and went in her life. It was exciting to meet her aunt and then she was gone.

Rainbow could still see the amazing Ninja eels (she was sorry to have had to cut one) and the lovely geisha mermaids.

Guy Guy licked the salt from her tears. His round sympathetic eyes made her laugh. Her arms went around him for a Mer hug and he neighed, happy to see her in a better mood.

Neptune made a huge spray and filled shell cups. He tossed cocoa beans into them. The treat was delightful.

Then he turned to Rainbow with a serious face. "Regarding your missing Mer School today, you will write an essay. Perhaps on meeting your Aunt? Turn it in with a request for a pardon."

Rainbow wanted to roll her eyes or at least flounce her tail, if it didn't earn her months with no eel screens.

Resigned, she rolled over and over in Neptune's wake and swam down the water tunnel shortcut to the Coral Castle.

That evening, after Glendora's tasty kelp cakes with spicy ink sauce, Rainbow went to her room to write her essay. No point in putting it off. The wall screens were probably already out of her control. Just to see, she went to the billowy surface and pressed the embedded crustacean. The wall remained as it was. Deep! She swore to herself. At least if Bowrain shared in the punishment, she'd have some company. There was nothing she liked less than having to write an essay, unless it was reading them.

The coral ledge between her and Bowrain's waterbeds, held the twins' eel powered mer mind unit. Rainbow felt for a circular lever and flipped it up. Instantly, a fluorescent green screen with bright violet undertones appeared on the smoothed coral surface.

She visualized the prancing geishas and jumping ninjas and Aunt Yoshiba on her throne, fierce as her father.

Rainbow pressed her fingers in indentations and Oceanus net appeared on the screen. With her trident, now pencil length, she drew her aunt's silhouette, ending with the curls of long tendrils. She entered the image into the net by pressing an indented wavy line. Instantly, her aunt's face appeared on her eel-mail; beautiful strong, if not quite nice. "Aunt," she asked, "Can you tell me about your life?"

The ghastly green screen warmed with growing plum light, as the eel-mail went to her aunt's address. It curled back a length of eel video, Slowly the video unscrolled across her screen. Here was a young Yoshiba with legs, playing with a toddler Neptune in the shallow water of an island beach. A very beautiful face appeared close to the screen. Her mouth opened, full pinkish-red lips uttered the name CALYPSO! spelled out on the screen.

Calypso was both a colorful dark-skinned woman and

a woman with pale moon-white skin. She wore an orange red gown or was it a green-blue tunic? Was her hair yellow gold or pitch black—violet or turquoise? Calypso was all these things at the same time, as she danced to changing music and swung her children in the air. She played with them, never still—always one thing or the other.

"Your grandmother, Calypso was confusing, always shifting from one form to another," said Yoshiba. "Only Zeus could tame her, for a while."

"Grandpa! Did you ever meet him!" asked Rainbow excitedly.

Tears squished against the inside of Rainbow's screen, though it may have been rain. "Invisible," said Yoshiba, "except for a mega storm. There was thunder and lightning, when he left." Rainbow saw toddler Neptune make for the water. Yoshiba, fast as her chubby legs could go, threw herself after him.

Calypso was quick. Yoshiba's legs became tentacles and Neptune's a fin.

"So we could follow each other," Yoshiba said. "But, when we looked back at the shore, mom was gone! Calypso left us a song."

"What kind of song?"

"A funny song that brought her smile and smells from our island. Whenever we went too far, we heard and smelled our way home. Mom was always about, guiding us, though not in her body."

"Where is Calypso now?"

Yoshiba shrugged, "Everywhere, nowhere, I don't know,

exactly. She's a tune on the wind."

The eel screen lost connection and Rainbow found herself thinking about her mysterious grandmother and the invisible Zeus. *Maybe that's why dad is everywhere at once and nowhere too long, thought Rainbow.*

Am I the same? Rainbow began her essay, entitling it: YOSHIBA AND ME. She wrote about how she met her aunt, described her kingdom, as well as her aunt's memories and how lonely she was in her squid kingdom. Rainbow decided that once a week she would eel-mail her aunt about Merschool. It would be great fun to have news about the ninjas and geishas. she wanted to know more about her family.

That night she gave Neptune her essay. He read and pondered, stroking his beard. "Do you think I'm unpredictable?" he asked.

Rainbow rolled her eyes, "Are you ever!"

A storm gathered on his brow. "But you know I am always here!"

"Even if you're not?" "You're Mer!"

"Oh, Dad, I know you're around, even if you're not here. You know I love you."

Rainbow put her arms around him. "My fusty old Neptune dad!" Neptune sputtered with embarrassment, dissolving the storm clouds in the distance.

That night as she lay down in her waterbed, Rainbow couldn't get the shifting images of Calypso out of her mind. She could hear Bowrain's even breathing and tried to synch herself with her twin. Then she heard a faster beat, music from warmer waters, funny and sweet. She smelled pungent cinnamon and clove spices; heard a laugh and felt a breath of citrus on her cheek. A light kiss—was she asleep?

Rainbow saw the changing features of her itinerant, wandering grandmother. Eyes like Neptune and a smile she recognized, like her own.

CHAPTER 7

In the Queendom of the Mini-Mermaids

Pinky Onyx awoke in her tiny shell cradle and gazed up at her big sister Emerald.

"So where did you find me and when?"

"Rainbow found you in a jelly fish but this is where you came from," said Emerald, showing her a stringy seaweed sack. It was like the black "purse" that nestled baby stingrays, yet it was green and porous. Emerald had preserved it between two pieces of coral.

"You hatched from one of these. You were probably very small, less than half a digit," said Emerald, showing Pinky a small square on her own little finger.

"Now I'm the whole finger," said Pinky. "Is that where you came from?

"Sapphire and I came from Glendora's body." "And I didn't?"

"You were floating on the border of our waters."

"Can you take me there?" Emerald looked pained.

"You are my sister," said Pinky, and she kissed Emerald's palm, where she sat. "I am curious about the waters in which you found me."

"I will show you," said Emerald. "Stay close."

Pinky swam alongside her big sister, out of the window of the Coral Castle, past the anemones garden where she waved to old friends. Many a colorful night Pinky had nestled in their soft midst, past neighing seahorses eager to give rides to Neptune's daughters.

"I'll see if Guy Guy will take us to the border waters, " Emerald suggested, as she and Pinky reached the stables. (Rainbow might be Boy Boy's master in name, but in truth seahorses did as they liked.)

And so Boy-Boy, the chocolate colored seahorse with banana spots, took off; Emerald, attached to his side by ropes of her green hair, Pinky comfortable in his mane.

Eventually, they came to the border of Neptune's kingdom, the end of his royal-blue-indigo colored waters. The other side was iridescent purple pink.

No bigger than Emerald's pinky finger, odd I was found in these waters, thought Pinky Onyx, as they stopped at the border waters. There they were to bid farewell to Boy Boy. His concerned seahorse eyes looked seriously at Pinky and Emerald.

"In my species, we are both father and mother. Take care until you're back in your father's realm." His sensitive nostrils quivered. "I don't feel danger but you are in strange waters. I'll wait at the border."

"You don't have to do that," protested Emerald. "I'm sixteen."

"And I'm no baby, at fourteen," said Pinky. "I'm small

but I can see what's going on and then some."

"You are not krill."

"Certainly not!"

"And I'll make sure no fish makes a mistake," Emerald assured the worried seahorse.

"Still, I will busy myself in this region." Boy-Boy threw his head back proudly, a steed worthy of Neptune's stables. Ready to aid his young charges, yet he understood their need to swim free.

Side by side, Emerald and Pinky swam. Occasionally Emerald invited Pinky aboard her tail. There were striations in the water, ribbons of gray sea plants that looked like streamers. After a while, Emerald stopped trying to peel them off and let them adhere to her body. She looked a gray stripped mermaid, thought Pinky, now securely bound to her sister. Pinky closed her eyes and enjoyed the ride.

Where to, wondered Emerald, looking around her. She was beginning to tire and had yet to see their destination.

"When will we be there?" asked Pinky.

"I know no more than you. But one thing is certain. You cannot be one of a kind."

Then a downward pull. More streamers, gray sea plants twisted round and round their bodies. They were pulled downward, descending to a strange whirlpool. Four distinct points, like a crown, thought Emerald, as her bound body revolved ever faster with a powerful suction. Helpless, they hit churning waters. "Ow," winced Emerald as her hair painfully tightened. It will be pulled out!

"We don't treat visitors like that," said a bell-like voice with great authority. The maelstrom halted. *The most perfect mini-mermaid,* thought an amazed Emerald and Pinky. She wore a small crown trailed with the same gray streamers.

"Pardon our visitors' entrance. We do well to keep out large fish."

Emerald was unsure what the queen was saying, but she tried to bow best she could. Bound by gray streamers, she ended sitting respectfully on her tail. The mermaid queen flicked a trident the length of an eyelash and Pinky was free. She bobbed an awkward curtsey, which the Queen gracefully returned. Pinky was surprised by the gesture and the sweet tones the mini mermaid Queen used in addressing her, though Pinky had no understanding of her language. Then the queen pointed her trident and Emerald was free, muttering, "Thanks for thinking of me."

The Queen appeared emotional, yet contained and regal, thought Pinky in admiration. *Curious that she acts moved to meet me?* Then the Queen spoke to her in Mer. "Neptune's daughter and my own! It has been many a year since I saw my esteemed husband."

This information shocked Emerald, who blurted out, "The same Neptune as my father?"

"King of the Sea," affirmed the small queen. "He is also king in these waters where there are no mermen, only maids." She pointed to a row of seaweed pouches like Pinky's. There are new ones about to hatch in their time."

At the bottom of one, a squalling merbabe the size of a single fish egg was wriggling. Pinky was amazed by the miniscule babe. "What do you feed her?"

"Seahorse milk," said the Queen, handing her a small hollow tube, an eel fossil. "We put this in the babe's mouth, they can suck right away." With care, the Queen eased the child out and called for a full tube. Just as the new mer babe's gurgle was about to turn to a roar, the tube splashed down from the whirlpool. The Queen popped it into the babe's mouth. Her tail happily moved back and forth, until she fell asleep in the Queen's arms. More bell-like tones, and another mini mermaid appeared. The Queen was about to give the babe to her, when she saw Pinky's yearning.

She smiled, "But of course. You would want to be close to your own kind." She put the babe in Pinky's arms. *Never had Pinky seen a creature so beautiful.*

The Queen embraced Neptune's daughters, "You must meet your sisters. Tonight there will be a special celebration. The daughter lost has now come home. Rest up!"

"What are you called?" asked Pinky. "Meribe."

"I am Pinky Onyx."

After the nurse mini-mermaid came for the babe, Pinky and Emerald were shown a room that breathed. The walls were made of soft billowy material, like the inside of the gills of a huge fish! As the room exhaled, Pinky and Emerald found themselves yawning to the same rhythm.

They rolled over into clam beds lined with the same soft material. Pinky and Emerald massaged their hard scales against the clams. It was pleasant to scrub off barnacles and seaweed after their long journey. When Emerald rolled toward Pinky for a "good night," she was already asleep. *Comfortable, this place is natural to her,* thought Emerald, before she succumbed to the gentle undulations of the clam bed.

In what seemed no time, Pinky awoke to light filtering into the gill room. Bright shimmers caressed her eyelids. She crawled onto Emerald's tail and twirled around, laughing.

Emerald was annoyed to be awakened, but seconds later she was charmed by the bell-like tones of mini-mermaids singing amid shell cymbals and trumpets. As Emerald and Pinky wondered about the source of the music, the billowing walls evaporated. In the distance on a high coral shelf, mini mermaid singers and musicians made music, enthralling an audience of bottom feeders, mollusks and barnacles, crabs and other crawlers of ocean beds.

Pinky thought she'd like to be closer. Immediately before her, on a flat wall of water, appeared her listening image close to the musicians. She put her finger on the image and the wall broke like a bubble. Emerald and Pinky merged with the actual scene.

The music of the mini-mermaids was like nothing they had ever heard. Emerald, a noted singer in Neptune's orchestra of talent, had not the ability of mini mermaids..

Each focused on a group of notes. Together they created a spectrum of sound that undulated and caressed the ear and emotions.

Tears flowed from Emerald's eyes, as though she was released from all sadness, new as the morning sun. Pinky

found her sometimes dark thoughts, that she was an out-
sider both in the Coral Castle and with the minis, was gone.
Much as the water and sky were separate realms joined
together by Earth, she was part of both realms. With new
eyes, she looked at Emerald and felt the love of equals.
Emerald was bigger, older and wiser. But Pinky, was wise
and loving enough to see Emerald was not more perfect.

Pinky was somehow unsurprised, when the Queen of
the Mini-mermaids met her with outstretched arms. Pinky
entered her embrace and truly felt she was home. When
she raised her head, the Queen was also crying. "Your maj-
esty, why the tears?"

"I am thinking of your father and our love so long ago."

"Do you miss him so terribly?"

"Neptune is king of all the oceans. You cannot swim
through a wave and not feel him nearby. You can't feel the
storm churn the depths without knowing his anger. His
fears appear in the overcast sky, that clears instantly to
cloudless blue. So his love for me has never waned. It is
eternal, though I am not."

"Is that why he has two families?"

"He is father of all the creatures in the sea, not just our
families."

I may be lucky to have his name, thought Pinky, but he
angers too easily. "He can be bossy and know-it-all," she
said.

"I didn't say he's without fault," said the Queen. "But he
has my love and Glendora's. I rejoiced when he wed her.
But even in favored waters, his melancholy is vast as his

kingdom."

"Does this mean I have two mothers?"

"Always," said the Queen, "and two castles and two beds. Do you not recall your days as Rapture?"

Pinky shook her head and thought how the name seemed an old memory, a part of herself only vaguely recollected. "Will you visit?" she asked, anxious not to lose this familiar mother recently found.

"When Glendora feels as kindly as I do, I will come."

"How do you know how Glendora feels?"

The Queen took Pinky's hand and swam with her to her chambers in the bubble palace. Inside was a basin made of old brass found on a ship. When she looked inside, she could see Glendora's room and her dear mother, pensively gazing at the anemone garden.

"I can read her thoughts, because mermaids have a common mental wavelength. We are part of the same psychic entity. The hard part is to be able to pick out individuals."

"Does Glendora know you exist?"

"She knows about the race of mini-mermaids. She doesn't want to know that Neptune has another mermaid family. Yet she recognized you as his daughter and accepted you into her family."

"Is she jealous of you?"

"That is not possible. She is a Queen! Though by nature she is not the sharing type of mermaid," explained the Queen. "Look deeply into the basin."

Pinky wished Glendora would come and pick up her own basin. Not surprisingly, she did just that. Her eyes looked into Pinky's magnified by the water between them.

Glendora's pensive expression changed to love and wonder. "Pinky Onyx! I am glad you called home! Is Emerald with you?"

"Yes, but not at this moment," Pinky answered.

"Where are you?"

"In the Queendom of the Mini-mermaids," said Pinky. "They are our kin."

Glendora's glance was evasive.

"There is someone I want you to meet."

The Queen's face joined hers at the basin. Pinky felt a little nervous as the two Merqueens stared unsmiling into each other's eyes. Then an image swam to life in the basin, Neptune's shaggy head. He laughed his hearty laugh, and the Queens felt the same love coming from him. With a quick glance at Glendora, he dived back down to whatever depths he had risen from.

Glendora was formal. "Thank you for safeguarding my daughters . "

The Queen was equally formal, "It has been a pleasure to meet our daughters."

"I hope that we will also meet some time."

"If destiny wills it," said Glendora, meaning she was equivocal.

Queen Meribe bowed and withdrew from the basin. "Pinky Onyx, when are you coming home?" asked

Glendora.

"When destiny wills it," said Pinky with a smile.

"You are fresh, my child!"

"Mom, a couple of days! Emerald is investigating the choir here. " Pinky pleaded.

"I guess we could use some changes," Glendora said.

"The small mermaids, join in one sound, groups of them, taking different notes. It's pretty great. Sounds like they are one instrument!"

Glendora's hand floated through the basin. Pinky's lips brushed it and Glendora was gone.

The world of the mini mermaids was unfamiliar to Glendora. She assumed they were charming. Undoubtedly the Queen was so, and yet Neptune's life with her was before he met Glendora. Obviously she supplied something missing. Probably a long length of tail, she thought with satisfaction. Hers flapped behind her, lavender in the light of late afternoon. Neptune was what humans called a serial monogamist. Currently, he was married to her. She was happy with that thought, until she remembered his face in the basin.

She didn't want to know about his visits to the mini kingdom. But it was very good for Pinky to see her size as normal, even if it meant some day she might leave the Coral Castle. A situation, she didn't want to consider now.

Glendora glided to the pantry off the dining area of the Coral Castle. There were too few of her family to cook for tonight.

Just Bowrain and Sapphire, Neptune would come later. He had to inspect a new shipwreck, an oil tanker near the Indian Ocean. For once, his conscience was clear. The sinking was not due to inclement weather, sudden storms, but a rival tanker. Men aboard had engineered a leak. By the time Neptune arrived, the spill was already concentrated, ruining his reef. He spread the oily stuff with winds, spraying drops as far as possible. It was desperate work. Fish and fowl alike would gasp for breath. Bodies slick as his own could falter.

Glendora went out to Sapphire's garden to see what anemones and algae she might gather to counter the awful substance. She filled a tub with them, awaiting the return of her noble king. Then thought again of dinner.

CHAPTER 8

The Idyll of Charlie and Sapphire on Long Beach Island

Glendora Onyx worried about her children in the off-hand fatalistic way of Merkind. She hoped Rainbow's adventure – seeking and Sapphire's yearning for romance didn't cause them great unhappiness. Glendora wanted to protect but not interfere with her children's growing abilities. The problem was adventures held danger and only Bowrain and Emerald had the sense to recognize it. Rainbow was a daredevil, who would go to the edge of mermaid existence just to see the other side. Sometimes Glendora stood in for destiny, if she could. But her children had grown enough to block her sight. She wasn't at all pleased with this sign of maturity.

Today she would help in Sapphire's garden and bring home the best fare for Neptune's dinner. But first she wanted to check on her children. Who knew what trouble they had found?

With a deep sigh, both wanting and not wanting to know, Glendora poured clarity water from her special crystal flask into the deep silver basin. The flask was useful and beautiful, like most of Bowrain's presents from the ocean floor. Her bureau was crowded with glass doorknobs she used to decorate her scales and silver tridents humans called forks, which glinted in her hair. In fact, Bowrain had recovered so many tridents, that Neptune gave them as favors to those who did him service.

Her favorite gift, perhaps the loveliest of all, was a huge milky white moonstone. Like most mermaids, she had second sight but it was capricious; sometimes true, sometimes not. With the stone, the future was a solid vision. Her knowledge was a useful curb for Neptune's impetuous pronouncements. No matter how idiotic, he believed what he said, though on occasion he did consult her and change his course.

Glendora peered into the depths of the silver basin and saw Sapphire not in her garden, but sitting on a rock on a beach combing knots from her long blue hair. High above her, on a wooden walkway, was a huge metal wheel turning in the sky. A short distance on the walkway, a man fed flames into his mouth. *Sapphire was in plain sight! What could she be thinking of? Was she trying to attract human attention,* worried Glendora, when a young boy, came to the rock.

"Charlie!" Sapphire exclaimed, "I've come again."

The human boy knelt in the sand and took her hand. "I want you to stay with me, for a while," he said.

His eyes were adoring. Sapphire's smile met his. Like a big sister, thought Glendora. She had Bowrain, what appeal had he?

"I will build you a home and visit you every day.

Please come with me."

"Where? The place where people walk on boards?"

"A quiet place, Long Beach Island," said Charlie. There are small islands and marshes. Some are protected."

"You mean Neptune watches them?"

"No. Fisherman and builders can't disturb the wildlife."

"Am I wildlife?"

"Are you ever," said Charlie.

Sapphire slipped from her rock and swam out to the waves.

Charlie stood sadly on the shore. "Come on in!" Sapphire called.

"I am not as good a swimmer as you." "Can you ride?"

Charlie looked up in awe, his answer to a secret wish.

"Let's go then!" Sapphire rode a wave to where he stood.

Tentatively, Charlie slid so he straddled her tail. "Slippery. How do I hold on?"

"My shoulders. And whisper directions. I'll only dive if we're followed."

"And I'll only drown if you dive?"

"No, Charlie," said Sapphire. She kissed his cheek.

You will see."

Charlie climbed on Sapphire's iridescent blue back, held onto her shoulders. He gave her instructions to follow the shoreline. As they swam away from Coney Island, Glendora thought once again, *"What is Sapphire doing?*

Water was their medium. Glendora put her head inside

the basin and thought directly to Sapphire. "Leave the boy on shore and come home!"

"Mom, I'm almost grown-up. I can make some decisions!"

"Sapphire, you know the rule about contact with humans."

"Mom this is a learning experience. I'm making a friend. Bye!"

Glendora cursed the fact that Sapphire at sixteen had enough maturity to mask her thoughts. They were as opaque now, as the water in the basin.

Young Charlie could not believe the speed of mermaid travel. Her body was untiring and their minds were as one. Dive was a thought. Before he could wonder about breathing, the cheek she had kissed sprouted gills. When they surfaced, he navigated through maze-like marshes filled with white egrets and black crows. Sapphire chirped the greetings of both birds. In an inlet, crabs in mud holes hailed Neptune's daughter, ignoring the human astride her back. Too many kin were hunted and boiled by humans.

"Not my fault," said Charlie. "I went crabbing once and we threw them back." No deception, Sapphire realized, her temper cooling. She pulled herself onto the shore, dumping Charlie off her back. She needed a rest. While Sapphire closed her far seeing eyes, Charlie explored. He found some rusty rods and lines in the shack. Outside, he noticed the sagging roof and a spare board to prop it up. Sapphire heard sounds of wild life, pelicans, ducks, ocean seals miles away. She made harsh honking sounds and listened to answers.

"What will you need to stay in the shack?" Charlie asked.

Sapphire looked at him strangely, "I don't live inside." A phalanx of egrets greeted her and the fish and crabs from the mud. A pelican carried in his mouth a large pink comb missing many teeth. Sapphire began to work on the knots in her hair. She practiced scales of song that put her in touch with the wind, lightning. The weather was Neptune's communication system.

"What are you doing?" asked Charlie.

"Letting my father know where I am. He likes me to be in touch but he leaves me alone."

Charlie sat beside her. He took her hand in his and turned it over. It was smooth and white as a shell. *Unearthly* he thought. *More beautiful than a human hand.* "I live nearby, by bicycle."

"Now that your weight is off my back, I'm free to swim."

"When will you be done?" asked Charlie, kicking a rock. Suddenly he realized, *she could go wherever. Was this a waking dream?*

"When I am," she said. And with a flip of a royal blue tail, Sapphire disappeared into the swamp, moving rapidly toward the clear bay. Can I have a lift home!" Charlie called.

The big fin stayed in the air a long moment. A grinning Sapphire resurfaced, her hair so blue black it looked almost purple. "Lucky for you I wasn't far."

She held still, while Charlie got on her back. In the lovely dusk light, secure on her scales, he thought he had never been so happy.

Sapphire swam Charlie to his house in Long Beach Island, a beach cottage dwarfed by new mansions. "Farewell, until tomorrow!"

"What can I bring you?"

"I have water. You will come back? "

"Every day after school."

"If you forget I will be gone."

"My mother worries when she doesn't know where I am."

"So does mine."

"Really? You have a mother?"

"Do I look like a hatchling?" asked Sapphire with a mocking sound like baby ducks.

Charlie danced home and got his bike out of the garage. He made figure eights in the asphalt street.

The next morning was Sunday. When he heard the doves on the roof, he awoke. His mother had left a note about fishing with friends. He took his cell phone as always, packed peanut butter and jelly, some bread, his pillow and fish flakes from his Aquarium. He took off on his bike to the shielded inlet. As he rounded the corner where the road stopped and the bog began, Charlie decided to stow his bike.

The curve, where the road stopped, was covered by tall yellow-green marsh grass. The bike hidden, he waded through the spongy areas that led to the shack. The ground was filled with crab holes, muddy and spongy. More bog water than mud, he wondered about a more direct route, when through the viscous water, he saw the glint of a huge fish tail.

At the same moment, he heard a beautiful song. A bird in harmony with its surroundings. But something alien in the sound, a strange quality. Words became intelligible, as the mermaid sang:

"Charlie from the beach cottage comes to visit me. He's brought a pillow for my wet head, fish flakes, and sandwiches for he. I will show him reef and sea. We will play in the water, we."

"Sapphire! Wait! It's slow going."

Soon he was holding her cool shoulders, as she dived below the surface, toward the road end, where he had stowed his bike.

She ducked behind the grass, as he retrieved his stuff and returned to his mermaid ferry. The pillow behind her shoulders was comfy. He strapped his food provisions in a day pack around his waist and soon fell asleep. He came to on the grass before the hut with his soggy pillow. On crabbing cage tables were peanut butter and jelly sandwiches.

The mermaid urged him to eat. She opened her mouth to show him the inside, smooth like a fish with pointed shark-like incisors. Peanut butter would just gum the works, she said. Charlie fed her spoonfuls of the jelly and small pieces of bread. She enjoyed them with flecks of fish food.

She made him throw the lobster traps out in the marsh. And, when they were sitting deep in the water, she made peculiar frothy gurgling sounds.

"Indigestion?" he asked. "No, I am digesting!" "Can I take your photo?" "No, it's forbidden." "Will your dad find out?"

"It's electronic?"

Sapphire made him return his cell phone to his pocket and then, all was forgotten in the excitement of the moving traps. When they pulled them up, there were many live lobsters.

Unlike the crabs he had seen in the pails or the poor lobsters with rubber banded claws in the fisheries, these seemed happy to be in her traps. Claws were waved, as she joyfully greeted them in Mer and the cages opened. Charlie moved back, unsure of these excited creatures.

When Sapphire sang her odd frothy song, they moved and clicked time with their claws in a dance.

"Dance the crab," Sapphire instructed him.

So Charlie imitated their slow clicking movements. Back and forth, side to side, as they clicked claws with partners and then changed. Sapphire, his partner, sat on the marsh grass, thumping her tail in the water. Exhausted, he sank beside her, as their lobster friends slipped back into the inlet.

When he awoke, feeling mucky and chilled, he realized he was alone. He also realized his mother would have called.

Charlie felt for his cell phone in his pants pocket but

it was waterlogged and unusable. The sun was long gone. Was it, 6:00? It was fall and still got light early, except it wasn't light. It must be late.

"Sapphire," he called. "I have to go home." "STAY," came the reply. "I am here. STAY." "What about my mother?"

"Bother your mother. Don't you want to see the moon?"

"Is it full tonight? Do you do something weird on full

WHEN *Sapphire sang her odd frothy song, they moved and clicked time with their claws in a dance.*

moons?"

"No. But fish are up and about. We can swim with them. I can take you."

Before Charlie could protest, Sapphire placed him in front of her. She held his back so his head was above water. "Now my cell phone will never work," he thought, until she kissed his ears, which changed to gills. No longer did he blink water out of his eyes. He was swimming with sideways sight, like the other fish.

A swordfish greeted him, as spawn of the mermaid. He was annoyed at first, but then kind of liked his new self. Sapphire and Charlie passed a school of minnows, who spelled out greetings in silvery patterns. A dignified old marlin nodded severely and silly cat fish flicked their whiskers back and forth.

Water felt soft and Charlie was tired, so he just enjoyed the motion and didn't know how long he and Sapphire sailed the bay. He found himself full of mud in his own bed. His mother opened the door.

"CHARLES! Where were you last night?"

"You would never believe me, he muttered.

Looking at crabs, mom! I got lost getting back.

Sorry! I'll wash this stuff."

"Just wash yourself. School's in an hour!"

While the tub filled, Charlie peeled off his mud-caked clothing and eased himself into the warm clean water. *What a strange dream, swimming with her,* he thought. Then he saw an iridescent blue scale on the white bathroom tile. He reached for it. *Hard enough for a guitar pick,* he thought, and held it to his eye. Charlie saw Sapphire's laughing face.

He could barely wait for the school day to end. He found his bike and rode speedily to the inlet. Charlie let out a cry, like a heron. A return one made him look toward the sky. A good mimic of herons, pelicans, crows and doves, Charlie answered calls without understanding. But this Heron answered him! "Come see me. Dinner awaits!"

Charlie thought, *dinner with my mermaid!* He saw, Sapphire at the shack, where she had laid out large shells for dishes. She was considering how to decorate the lobster trap, which served as a table. She found sprigs of purple heather and placed them in squares between the boards. Her hands moved fast, weaving the flowers.

"Just in time!" she greeted him in heron chirps, back and forth sounds between her and the real birds. Charlie was astonished. He was sure she understood the language. He smiled, embarrassed, and sat on another trap. Sapphire, sprawled on the grass, looked at him fondly. Then focused on the inlet. Charlie felt a tug at his fingers and looked down. A mischievous crab had his fingers in a claw. Charlie tossed it off and Sapphire giggled. Suddenly, she upended her table, and dove into the swamp. An instant later, she returned with a fish and put the wriggling creature in his lap. "You can eat," she said earnestly. He says his time in this place is at an end."

Charlie looked at the live fish making wet marks on his jeans and wondered what to do. "I actually prefer seaweed," he said. "Can you tell him it's nothing personal? I appreciate it."

He thought there was something grateful in its eye, as Sapphire flipped the fish back in the marsh. She grinned her inscrutable mermaid grin and flipped her own fish body onto the marsh grass and wriggled to a convenient rock.

"A brush, comb and a mirror," he said bringing them from his knapsack.

"Why thank you!"

"What's that beverage?" he asked, pointing to a little bottle.

"Dew. It tastes best fresh," she said. "Drink up." Charlie found it musty but figured that was the bottle.

"Best I ever had," he said politely.

"Here's your dried up seaweed. I made it last night," said Sapphire. "Not as good as from my garden, but I'm working with what's here."

Charlie took a small bit. *Not so bad, salty and smelly.* "Okay," he said cheerfully.

"You lie," laughed Sapphire, "but I did feed you." Then she called to the inlet. Egrets, herons and a group of crabs circled her fins. A huge crab sat in front of her and made crabby gestures."

"What's that about?" "Not for your ears!"

"Really. I don't like being left out."

"They wondered about human stew," she said with a look that made Charlie uncomfortable. "I didn't share their wonder. But I guess fair is fair."

"I don't eat crab."

"Of course, you throw them back."

"I was with other people, Sapphire."

And soon Charlie was sitting his arms around her fish-tail, as she stroked his cheek. He stayed there until the sun came up in the marshes and two dreary words came to him; SCHOOL, HOMEWORK.

He quickly figured out a cover story; a friend to say he spent the night, the homework done in recess. And though his mom looked at him strangely, she didn't interfere. Charlie knew she wanted him to become more independent and was trying to grant him more privacy. Whatever, thought Charlie, as long as he could see his mermaid. He must be careful not to overstep the rules. It would ruin everything. (In truth, though he put it out of his head, he didn't like deceiving his mother.)

Between Charlie and Sapphire a routine developed. It seemed she was as dependable as his mother, without the scolding. She waited for him and was glad to see him, but there the resemblance ended.

His mother was predictable, whereas Sapphire was always devising new adventures. Then both talked a lot. Sapphire went on about her garden. She loved the anemones of every color, so unlike the always-green marsh grass. But the grass wasn't bad, as background for the stark white egrets.

In the dark of late night, she took him to areas of the marsh, where plants germinated and fish spawned. "New life!" Sapphire said. Through her sight, he saw tiny bursts of energy, as creatures came into being. *A sun in a tiny cosmos,* Charlie thought. He liked their excursions less, when she left him in some *weird place and he had to fend for himself, until she returned. Did she just forget?*

"You sure you're not taking me to my death?" he asked angrily after one such excursion. Sucked into a bog and stabbed by a swordfish was not his idea of fun.

"Do you think I thought about that?" she retorted.

"Humans can't take a joke," she pouted. "It's the problem of your race. Well, now you're rescued."

Charlie didn't like her attitude. Usually Sapphire was fun, though unpredictable. It was tiresome not to know where you were going or what would happen. And what good was it to have your own private mermaid, if you couldn't tell anyone about her?

He had a friend, a girl named Joyce from library, who wanted to meet Sapphire.

"Not a good idea," he said, but then Joyce followed him after school.

Sapphire pounced on the little girl and held her head in the water. "What's this, Charlie?"

"Joyce! Please don't drown her!"

"Does she fish?"

"No, she's vegan."

"What?"

"Eater of vegetables," said Charlie and he grabbed at Sapphire's hands, until she let a spluttering Joyce crawl to the shore. Charlie followed.

"You've ruined everything," said Charlie. "Was she really here?" asked Joyce.

"You didn't see her?"

"Something was holding me down, but it could have been a giant squid."

Charlie looked at her quizzically, "Like we've seen them in these waters?"

"If one person sees it, it can be imagination. Two is different. You saw it, right?"

Charlie shook his head no. He had wanted to share his knowledge of mermaids. But now to explain Sapphire seemed a betrayal.

He walked Joyce home. But the next day Sapphire was gone and the one after that. Charlie went to the shack and tended Sapphire's plants, but she never came.

"I'm sorry," said Joyce. "I had no idea she was so touchy."

"You had no right to follow me."

"I was curious. You shouldn't have told me about her." Why did I have to show off, wondered Charlie.

That question haunted him and the secret he didn't keep. It was hers to reveal to whom she chose.

One bleak windy fall day, he saw a sign at the shack. A deep sea anemone, deep red in color, floated in a bowl of sea water. Another time, he found a lobster claw around an old mirror. That day he looked for new sea life in the deserted mud caves of the crabs.

Charlie heard a motorboat putt-putting from the inlet into the cul de sac. When it came to sight, he saw Joyce with two older boys with fishing gear. "No," he groaned.

"I just told my brother about this place. It seemed a

good bet for crabs."

"Wayne!" called Charlie, incredulous, "There's nothing here. Fished out."

Joyce waded out to the shore to join Charlie. He couldn't look at her. Wasn't coming once enough?

"Just Wayne and his friend, Josh. Mom was glad to get them away from the TV, fresh air and all that. Also a way for me to see you. You never talk to me in school now."

Charlie's mind was racing. If they crabbed there, who knew what could happen?

"Hey, Joyce. No mermaids here. No crabs. False advertising I think," called Wayne.

Wayne and Josh threw cans of soda overboard and Charlie heard a familiar silvery voice, "Here I am! Sapphire Onyx, daughter of Neptune, King of the Sea!"

He turned and saw a silver flash, a blur of scale and fin.

The only sounds were birds calling to Sapphire. Then Josh turned to Wayne.

"Did you see that?"

"No," said Wayne. "Joyce, did you see her?" "And what are you going to do about it?" asked Charlie.

"I could try to capture her and make a million dollars if she doesn't kill me," began Wayne.

"Or drag you to the deep," said Josh, "Isn't that what they do, tempt sailors to their drowning?"

Sapphire came up to the beach. She looked very bored.

"Show them your teeth!" said Charlie.

"Do you think I'm a trained shark?" asked Sapphire snippily. "And you two would make very poor fish food."

"I don't know if I can deal with this," said Jack. "Agreed," said Wayne, "Let's blame it on lack of sleep, too many videogames."

Sapphire disappeared into an inlet and made duck sounds.

"Wow, want some ducks?"

"We don't hunt, you fool. No guns or bows and arrows here."

"Right," said Wayne, "We fish."

"Want some crab traps?" asked Charlie, wading in to give them the traps.

Both boys liked the idea, baited the traps and threw them overboard. Charlie looked at Joyce triumphantly.

"What are you so pleased about?" "You'll see."

He gave Joyce a tour of the shack. While she wasn't Sapphire, for a human girl she knew a lot about cephalopods. As the sun went down, he realized he hadn't heard a sound from Sapphire or the boys. Then the wind changed. Two calling voices. He and Joyce went to the inlet, where they saw a comic sight. Wayne and Josh were stuck in the mud, traps on their heads. Crabs were on their hands and feet.

"Sapphire!" called Charlie at the pitiable sight. The two boys were crying and calling for help. But no silvery voice replied.

Charlie and Joyce waded into the muck and released their heads from the traps. They also got their share of crab bites. Then Charlie went to the shack and returned with cloth and buckets.

"Crabs, don't you know me? I'm Sapphire's human friend."

The crabs pretended not to know him but they stopped biting. Charlie was able to release the boys, who shakily climbed into their boat.

"Joyce, please go. I want to be alone."

Joyce joined them in the boat. "Charlie are we friends? I had to come. Please forgive me."

"Joyce. We're friends. I'll see you tomorrow."

As a smile lit her intelligent face, Charlie felt happy he would see her tomorrow. He waited as night fell past dinnertime. Who cared that his mom would be angry?

When the moon was full, he took a mirror to a high rock and looked into it. He thought he saw the silhouette of a girl with long blue black hair.

"Sapphire. Can you forgive me?"

"For-give, forgive," called a pure white bird with deep blue eyes. As Charlie gazed into them, the bird changed into a mermaid sitting on a rock on the strip of shore below the shack. Charlie ran to her. He took her hand and held it for a long instant. No words. Loving feelings were between them.

CHAPTER 9

Bowrain's dental dreams and the cave time forgot

Bowrain's tooth hurt, the last bi-molar in the back. His mouth was open, held in place by two smooth mussel shells, while Dr. Murk, his dental lobster, lectured Bowrain. Water termites were consuming his teeth. The sticky sweet hibiscus jelly he loved was attracting them.

Bowrain closed his eyes, not wanting to see the green claw clamped around his long pointed tooth. Sea water sprayed as the claw cleaned, and Bowrain thought *I'd rather be asleep.* Dr. Murk heard him. A long tentacle of squid stuff went into his nerve and Bowrain cursed his weakness for the lovely jelly. Underwater hibiscus was a rarity, Sapphire cultivated in her garden. Glendora had offered him other treats, but somehow he couldn't resist. Dr. Murk said, "If you cleaned your teeth, this would not happen. Take time to do it well! "

Bowrain did not grunt an answer. His pain receded with his consciousness of reclining in Dr.Murk's giant clamshell, while he scraped off the termites. Bowrain was aware of his body in a larger way. He had huge biceps, deeply tanned skin and a weathered face. Older than eons, he looked at the world with a newborn's eyes. He stood upright in water to his waist. He held his arms out to the heavens, connecting both realms.

Electricity ran from heaven to earth, He was the instrument and it felt natural, because the sea was his kingdom. He belonged, calm in the ever-moving water around him.

Bowrain, sinewy arms raised, shouted at the heavens. Storm clouds crashed together, punctuated with bursts of lightning. He laughed joyfully, crunched his face up and gave a long loud bellow. More thunder echoed in the atmosphere. The sound carried through him and was amplified underwater.

He took handfuls of clouds, shaped them into balls and hurled lightning bolts. He jumped to catch one, made it larger, and shaped it into a boomerang. It sailed around the curvature of the earth, once, twice, then hit the water, churning up a huge maelstrom. He whirled into the center and flew on a geyser up to the heavens, roaring.

The clouds scuttled across the sky. He fell to the water, jumped up and down, made whirlpools. A thunderbolt boomerang came at his head. He ducked. A powerful whirlpool sucked his tail, chest, and head! He stabbed through the center into the bottom of the sea.

Too much commotion even for Bowrain, king of the sea! How was he to stop it? Water churned and seethed, a furious foamy mass. Agitated creatures, eels and swordfish, attacked his fins.

Bowrain kicked them off. Squawking creatures of the sky, birds pummeled and drenched in a violent icy storm. He felt small claws. The inquisitive gaze of a baby owl met his. Who? Said the Owl mournfully. *What*, thought Bowrain, as the claws became firmly embedded in his skull. He braced himself on his trident, "ENOUGH! I command you!" But the little owl did not budge. Bowrain shook his head yet could not dislodge him. His fins now slipped in a million whirlpools, while swordfish speared them. He danced to evade their thrusts. What was it to be King of the Sea? Why couldn't he halt, what he had set in motion?

Much better to be a slow moving sea slug on the bottom of the ocean, he thought. And he was wet, rolling over and over in the water. His actions were next to nothing.

"Ah, stay here," said Dr. Murk, who put Borain's head back in position.

Lucky, I'm just a kid, thought Bowrain sleepily. Let Dad do his job. But as he was feeling comfortable, waist high in water, a giant squid pulled him under and grabbed his fin. *No longer between heaven and sea bottom, how do I win?*

"Bowrain, I am done now," said Dr. Murk. "The termites are gone. Watch the jellies."

Bowrain staggered out of the dentist's clamshell and heard a voice, sweet and calming. A cool hand on his brow, then a strong arm under his shoulder. He was carried away to the softest possible material. He awoke in his bed in the Coral Castle. There was the lovely concerned face of his mother, Glendora. "Sleep, Bowrain. And don't sneak that candy!"

He wanted to smile but his mouth was numb. He looked with love at his mother and felt relief. Glendora smiled. She put a weightless hand on his forehead. His eyes closed. He was among the clouds, floating like the others. He drifted down to Rainbow in a clear sea. She considered the black entrance of a cave.

"Forbidden!" he hissed at Rainbow. "What are we doing here?"

"You saw the X," she answered smartly.

"I am asleep!" he began, interrupted by a sound, harsh and oddly muffled. *The source was not something with a palate or even a mouth*, he thought, intrigued. He pulled himself up the rocks outside the forbidden cave.

Rainbow looked at him. He knew her thought, *the red X, is visible only to Mer eyes.* That was more than a hint to go past.

The marking assured that humans would not be aware there was a cave. So clearly did the X hide the dark shape from any but Mer. Yet he could not squash an intense curiosity.

Above them, a pitched screeching and shaking of earth made the twins pause. They took another look into the cave. Thick steam filled the entrance. The waters must be very hot. Even the sun seemed closer to that cave. They watched huge creatures pass; a dinosaur-like fish, a giant squid, and a very gentle creature with four paddling legs and a dolphin head, which turned toward them.

"Bowrain," Rainbow began cautiously, these are not home waters."

Bowrain concurred, "Some kind of portal. I am not going in there...."

A thundering sound, a squeal, the gurgle of water.

Rocks fell into the entrance. "That's it for me," said Bowrain, sliding back into the water.

"You're scared," said Rainbow. "I'm not! Boys are such 'fraidy cats!" she laughed, launching herself into the hissing steam into the cave.

Maybe she knows something I don't? He wondered, finding his way after her. NO! He shouted. A round shelled creatures covered Rainbow in black ink.

Bowrain pulled his half conscious sister away from the creature. Gasping on the rocky ledge, her scales blackened and gunked and probably her gills, he wondered, *ink? How was he to get them back to the Coral Castle? If he could figure out what direction "back" was.*

Long gone were the familiar waters of the Coral Castle. Neptune's map had shown a loose circle of caves around the Coral Castle. The cave entrance shone in a sulfurous yellow light. Outside, Bowrain saw only an embryonic coral reef full of living creatures. Home was not in sight. And Rainbow was injured. He must get that oily stuff off her.

"Ancient Cephalopods," gasped Rainbow.

"Why are you talking about fossils?" said Bowrain. "Squid-like creatures living in shells. How fabulous! We have time-travelled. Look, the coral reef hasn't yet formed."

Bowrain might have found it fabulous, if a huge mouth with razor teeth was not upon them. He grabbed Rainbow and dived. When they surfaced, the rock they had rested on was gone with part of the cave.

Rainbow still had gunk in her hair, but could breathe.

Weird as she looked, he found it hard to believe she was so excited.

"We have seen them and they don't exist!"

"Well they did at some point, or we couldn't see them now," said Bowrain logically.

"That's because we are back in their time," said Rainbow. "Neptune wasn't here either."

"Why are we?" he began, starting to get really scared now. "And how will we get back?"

"Who knows," said Rainbow blithely, "what an opportunity to see the beginnings! I bet we get extra credit at Merschool!"

"Terrific," Bowrain said, in a foul mood, getting worse, as he viewed the sea dinosaurs hunting giant sharks and wondered where Mer creatures fit into the food chain. Then Rainbow gave a cry of fear. Entangled with her flippers was a long, flat, slithery, whitish-pink form.

It began to pull her inside the cave entrance. Holding her was not an option, since Bowrain must lose a tug of war with a creature that size. "Don't resist," he told Rainbow, "I'm with you."

"Easy for you to say!" she screamed, grabbing rocks with little success. Fast and relentless was her enemy. As they entered the cave entrance, Bowrain gave a horrified gasp.

There, coiled in on itself, was a huge, white wormlike creature with a vile looking beak-mouth. A tapeworm, he thought, appalled, but a prehistoric one, the scale of which he could not imagine in his worst nightmares! If he offered himself, would it coil around him and consume him, instead of Rainbow? There was no reasoning with such a creature.

Could it ingest them?

(The same thought gave the creature short pause.) And if the creature ate them, could they live inside without being consumed? Bowrain took his trident from his necklace. The fork grew. Protective rays covered his whole body. Rainbow was in the same process, though not quick enough for part of her tail fin. They were in the slimey insides of the giant worm. The trident kept his stomach acids from their bodies, but breathing was not so easy. Not enough water.

Bowrain thought, *no one will know how we died.*

Rainbow thought, *mom will find us.* Bowrain thought back, *You're right. Dad probably knows, too.*

What punishment they would incur for disobeying about the x'd caves? Whatever it was would be welcome to this situation. Amazing he could think of anything else, as they fell around the worm's insides as it left the cave.

A drink, Bowrain prayed, please take a drink! And with the drink came one of the dolphin-like creatures with paddle arms and a serpent-like body. A "Dolly" dinosaur, Bowrain remembered the name from school. A row of sharp teeth but only for roots. He was trying to think of a plan, but already, she was working her teeth on an area of the worm with thinner skin. The twins' tridents kept the stomach acids away from Dolly. Soon the worm was tossing with stomach ache, relieved as the three tumbled out of its side.

Bowrain and Rainbow followed the affable Dolly to the surface waters outside the cave, a prehistoric world of giant swimming dinosaurs. Dolly treated the mertwins like her young, careful they dove and swam in her path. She ate schools of tiny fish and followed them to ever cooler open seas. Bowrain and Rainbow hugged her long neck. She was sad, leaving her young and looked long after them. They swam to the living coral reef that in several millennia would be their castle home.

Rainbow made a square window shape in the top of the living coral and climbed inside. She pulled Bowrain after her. "What is the point of this?" he began, when he realized he was again in his bed. And that Rainbow, her tail intact, was watching him sleep, next to the beautiful, concerned face of Glendora.

CHAPTER 10

Rainbow and Bowrain bring home Squidoo

Rainbow and Bowrain were surfing the waves on their tails, trying to see who could stay longer on the top of a twenty foot wave. Rainbow was on the top of a fifty foot wave, her tail fins victoriously waving at Bowrain. "Nah, nah, nah!" she crowed. Bowrain set his jaw. *He was better, more firmly in control than his flashy sister.* Sure enough, Rainbow got slapped down by a huge wave she didn't see coming. *Too busy doing her one-handed head-stand on the wave*, Bowrain smiled. He rolled in on that wave, perfectly balanced on his belly, cruising toward the shallows. Then he spotted a gray wispy-looking thing, tiny and vaguely transparent. He might have thought it was trash or a plant, until the creature fixed an eye on him. The other was closed. *A sad eye with a glimmer of hope,* thought Bowrain. He cupped the creature in his hands and shouted, "Rainbow, come here!"

Rainbow was not looking forward to her brother's gloating. Rare he could best her—the most agile of sea princesses! Yet he seemed preoccupied. Whatever with? Then she saw the yearning eye cupped in Bowrain's hands. "How did she survive uneaten?" At her words, the tiny squid cowered. She, Rainbow was sure it was female, made a small sound. Could she be old enough to know the language? The sound repeated. What did it mean? *Was the baby squid hungry?*

"What do you think it eats, anyway?" asked Bowrain. "It's a baby girl, not an it," sniffed Rainbow. "Whatever," said Bowrain. "I think she needs food on the double!"

Rainbow cupped her hands around her mouth and made high repetitive sounds, "Bulletin, Mer-wide web! Orphaned baby squid, sea cow needed!" A sea cow soon arrived. Bowrain welcomed the fish, which squirted milky stuff in a sea glass bottle. When it was full, the sea cow made a huffy exit, muttering doubtfully about the usefulness of feeding orphaned squids with her milk.

"She may be right," mused Bowrain. "It's not their regular chow."

"She's sucking it in," said Rainbow, as a white cloud of milk came back out.

"Mom will know what to do," said Rainbow. "Glendora doesn't let anyone go hungry," Bowrain agreed. "Let's go!"

"I can't swim and hold her at the same time!"

Bowrain dived to the bottom of the ocean and dislodged an old pie tin. Rainbow scooped the baby squid into the tin and swam with one arm, holding it flat. *Awkward to swim like this,* thought Rainbow. Worse, fish were looking hungrily at the tin. Safer if the squid were somehow attached to her body. She found stiff marsh grass and sticky mud. Quickly, she made a tiny basket.

"What are you going to do with that?" asked Bowrain,

keeping the pie tin safe in his arms.

"You'll see," she said, taking some of the long grass and plaiting the basket into her hair. More like being a baby in her mother's pouch."

"Squid don't have their young in pouches."

Rainbow ignored him. She moved the baby squid to her basket, safe in thick mermaid hair. As Rainbow swam, a squid eye closed. The baby was fed and asleep. What an accomplishment! They had done it! Perhaps they could keep her?

"What will mom say?" asked Bowrain, echoing their mutual thought.

Glendora looked at the tiny creature in the basket. "Neither of you has ever taken care of a baby squid or any creature, including yourselves!" Then she looked at the twins' sad faces and smiled in an encouraging way.

"We'll make sure she's okay. We promise, so help us Neptune," they said. Their words were so earnest and heart – felt that Glendora could only sigh. She knew when she was beaten. *Well, we haven't had a baby around here for a while,* she thought, *now that Ruby is older won't be so much.*

"First a good bed for the night," she instructed the twins. Taking the woven basket from Rainbow's hair, Glendora looked at the still sleeping creature and mused, like all babies, so sweet asleep!

Bowrain swam out of the Coral Castle to Sapphire's garden. Predictably, Sapphire was raking barnacles out of the anemones with her expanded Trident. He asked her about a bed and she answered without pause, "Ask the sponges."

"Would you help a baby squid?" he began, to a patch of sponges in the garden. "She needs comfort. When we met, she was lost and alone."

Many of the sponges were unmoved. A few gracefully rippled their red orange surfaces, as though mindlessly tossed by the current. One ochre-colored sponge had a kind heart buried in her soft stuff. "I will help her, but she must not chew me."

Carefully, Bowrain swam with the sponge into the floaty walls of the bedroom he shared with Rainbow.

She soon followed with a shell and placed it in the center of the curving room, between their two waterbeds.

When the sponge spread itself comfortably in the shell, Bowrain settled the baby squid upon it. "It's giving you a soft bed. No biting!" The squid didn't respond. Maybe she didn't like being moved, worried Bowrain. Then Rainbow rocked the shell and sang the sweetest Mer lullaby of all, about the beginning of the oceans and the first creatures of Neptune—even squids!

Soon the baby spread her small tentacles in her comfy bed. She shut her eyes and...glowed! Rainbow excitedly telepathed Glendora, "Mom, she's glowing! Why does she glow?"

"Bioluminescent," explained Glendora.

"Meaning they glow by themselves without a light source," Bowrain added.

"Let's call her Squiddoo! Kid and squid," Rainbow clarified.

"Yes, let's call her that," Bowrain answered, because it seemed right. The next morning, Glendora swam in with breakfast for the baby squid. She slowly poured sea water with plankton and tiny fish into Squidoo's mouth. The baby gobbled and went back to sleep, satisfied.

"She's growing," said Bowrain to Rainbow weeks later, as they looked down at the shell. Squidoo had tripled in size and was beyond the sponge. Bowrain thanked the creature, which he returned to Sapphire's Garden. He and Rainbow elongated their tridents and scraped out the floor, making a shallow pond in their room. It was hard work. They paused before finishing and Bowrain had an alarming thought. "Rainbow, we never asked mom if it was okay to do this."

"Why bother?" she answered tartly. "She can see every-thing."

"She has been kind of scarce," he agreed, looking at the wall screen of their room. No postings from his mother had come through.

Now daily they poured baskets of small fish into the hol-lowed-out pond and Squidoo eagerly pursued her meals. The twins felt great pride. "And mom didn't think we were responsible," said Rainbow.

"At least about this," agreed Bowrain.

Squidoo swam close to their side of the pond and slapped her tentacles on the edge, her signal for Bowrain. He put his hands in the water, as playful tentacles wrapped around them. Rainbow dipped her hand inside and felt ticklish suction cups moving on and off her fingers. She giggled and Squidoo opened her eyes wide, a laugh if squids did that. Fondly, they played with their pet in the pond. All were batted and chased around by hands, tentacles, and fish tails.

Months later, they awoke to find Neptune waiting for them by the pond. Squidoo also waited, now grown half-in, half-out of the pond.

"It's time you let her go."

"But she's happy here," said Bowrain. "How do you know that?"

"Look at her, dad," said Rainbow. "We're the only family she's ever known."

"Precisely. Why it's time to let her go."

"She won't know how to find food and hide from those who want her for food," pleaded Bowrain.

"She'll be lonely," wailed Rainbow, displaying the family's knack for high emotion.

"I didn't say she'd be alone," said Neptune. "I'm not heartless." Then Rainbow intuited his intention.

"A Squid Ball?" she asked eagerly.

"A conclave, a meeting of the species," said Neptune. "She will be introduced and welcomed among her own kind. They have much to teach her."

Rainbow looked at Squidoo, lounging contentedly in half the pond. *Did her eyes look a little fearful, worried? Was she a bit lost and lonely?* Bowrain put his arm around her shoulder. "You don't know that she feels that way. We both love her but dad's right. We've done our job. Time for her to be a grown up. She has to learn about that, just like us at Mer school."

Rainbow and Bowrain went to the billowing wall of their room and crunched the crustacean control. The grimacing creature launched their transoceanic screen.

The billowing wall disappeared. In its place, visible at once, were the deep waters of the world's oceans.

Wavy circles appeared on the screen. They could select one body of water or all. Bowrain pushed the crustacean over multiple wavy circles, selecting all the world's oceans, as well as the oval and curvy circles for lakes and rivers. A blank space for a message appeared. What should they say?

Bowrain considered, *GIRL SQUID IN NEED OF FAMILY? No.* His hand on another not too friendly crustacean he wrote: NEPTUNE, KING OF THE SEA, REQUESTS YOUR PRESENCE AT THE FIRST EVER SQUIDOO EVENT R.S.V.P BY ELECTRIC EEL. PRINCESS RAINBOW AND PRINCE BOWRAIN @ THE CORAL CASTLE.

Wavy lines of writing appeared like seaweed or a school of fish on the screen. The message swam throughout the world's waters. Among these the invitation reached the pale greenish water of Victoria Falls, the black rivers of Timbuktu, the electric blue surface of Australia's Pacific and Indian Oceans, the mucky brown tributaries of the Amazon River, Long Beach Island's indigo ocean and the gray-green waves of Coney Island.

Delighted colossal and tiny squids, cuttlefish and Japanese gray blacks, glossy squids in the Indian Ocean, and natives from the turquoise waters off Florida's Gulf of Mexico were proud to receive Neptune's invitation. From shallows, coves and giant canyons on the oceans' bottoms, ripples of message caught in sensitive tentacles.

Floating message waves reached porous brains with a luminous image of Neptune, large and fierce, surrounded by lots of edibles. Good eats would be at this party. The day after tomorrow's tomorrow, when the dark moon was down, they would meet at The Coral Castle. Neptune's shallows were at the center of a secluded half – moon of caves.

Meanwhile, as squids were gathering from all over the world, those in the shallows a ways from the Atlantic City Aquarium heard more than one call. Neptune's invitation registered as a the call of a colossal being, who filled up earth and sky. He was majestic, a fierce solid being, though not oblivious of even small fish, shrimp, and scores of minnows floating by. The other invitation was from a young squid, not a baby, but too young to know to keep to the dark, away from human scrutiny. She just wanted to play, and no oldster seemed near to keep her from harm. Below the perception of the squids, a floating sponge watched Squidoo, though its ability to protect her was limited.

An old mother from the Aquarium squid tribe, who'd expelled her last stream of offspring, gave a tremendous hoot and swam bravely toward the light, knowing how tasty that little squid might appear to predators. Through numerous brightly colored silvery fishing lures that resembled squid, she searched for the young one—avoiding sharp hooks.

The old squid saw the young one playing with a sponge half her size, unaware excited little humans on the beach saw her! A female with yellow hair like baby mermaids but two clunky skin tubes instead of a tail, and a much younger male with the same tubes, moved fast. They tried to catch the little squid with a hard red container. Delighted with new playmates, she swam around the red container, in and out of their skin tubes.

Trouble came from a large human female. *Her young,* thought the old squid. Why did she scream with fear? The little squid did not like her sounds.

"A squid! Poison tentacles, stay away!"

Poor little squid, thought the aged one, as streams of black ink engulfed her and the human children. Was it possible to get the youngster out of this mess?

Squidoo had no idea how it happened! One minute she was having fun, the next someone's yelling and there's black stuff around her. The yelling creature seemed to think it came from her. Interesting but her playmates are gone, and then there's a bristly thing around her.

There were rope squares, a net around Squidoo. She was jolted out of the water into the air, startled to see sky and feel underneath her a hard slippery surface. She was in a pail and couldn't swim out.

Where's sponge, she wondered, bobbing alone. But she wasn't alone. Human faces surrounded the top of the bucket. And there were minnows in the water.

Human eyes were riveted to her, as she chased the minnows. But that night in the dark, she felt very sad. No sponge friend, no mer twins, and, of course, no other squids. She sensed the caring feelings of the old mother, just before she was imprisoned in the bucket.

No chance to meet her now. Squidoo was very sorry for herself, floating in a bucket prison inside the Atlantic City Aquarium.

Why did Squidoo go out? Rainbow asked the sponge, now back in the Coral Castle. The sponge compressed its surface and then relaxed. The action made air sounds.

Rainbow understood. Squidoo wanted to feel water outside and see sky above the Coral Castle.

"Did you tell her the surface isn't safe?" asked Bowrain

"I tried but she moves fast . Got around me. You know babies," explained the sponge in old Mer.

"Indeed I do," said Rainbow, thinking of Ruby and poor Emerald. Bowrain also remembered their adventure with the giant baby in the cave.

"They like their own way," he said, "but also want an older person in charge. Good you stayed with Squidoo."

"Almost wish the humans took me too."

That night Rainbow borrowed Glendora's silver bowl.

She and Bowrain focused on Squidoo, until the waters cleared to show the Aquarium. She was the first to dive in, with Bowrain following. Soon they were outside the Aquarium.

"How do we get in?"

"And out," thought Bowrain. "The tanks inside don't seem to be connected to the ocean."

"I have a thought," said Rainbow, fingering her trident. "Second that thought," said Bowrain. They found an opening on the side of the building, a circle of concrete a little bigger than Rainbow's hand. She sniffed with distaste, "What is it?"

Bowrain put a finger in. "Water used by humans, not filled with wastes but stinks."

Rainbow made a face, "Lovely for Merfolk." Bowrain looked superior, "It won't kill you." "I am a princess," she said with obvious pride.

"AND I HAVE A SOLUTION!" they both thought at the same time. "That's the problem with being a twin," said Bowrain, "always having to share the glory." Rainbow shrunk herself with her trident and, for safety's sake, encased her form in a bubble. Bowrain followed suit. They emerged through the faucet in the mens' room and were seen in the mirror by a boy who exclaimed, "Can't be! When I look back, they won't be there!"

Bowrain was glad to oblige. He nodded to Rainbow and they swam into the pipe leading to an outside water fountain. The boy swiveled back. "Can sugar do that to you? I got to watch the soda…"

The mer twins peered out of the pipe, after the last toddler was held up for a drink. They spied Squidoo in a white bucket. A line of young humans were encouraged to touch a tentacle with the aid of an adult human. Both Squidoo's eyes were sadder even, than on the day they found her.

"Let's wait until they put this place to sleep," said Bowrain. Rainbow thought back, "yes," instead of signaling with her trident. They agreed. Attention from the humans was not a good idea.

Hours later, in the darkened room, they looked for Squidoo's glow, faint from fear and sadness. They let themselves into the bucket. At first, Squidoo thought they were something to eat. But when their bubbles wouldn't break, she recognized the tiny bell sound of Mer talk. A sharp feeling, the tiny prick of a miniscule trident, and she was as small as the twins; and as overjoyed to see them.

They also used a trident to make the white pail into a large cup, and put the now tiny Squidoo into it for the trip. Rainbow enclosed her in a protective bubble and the mer twins swam on either side, holding the cup with the half-grown squid small as baby krill. Out the pipe they swam toward their salt water home, the sea. A swipe of tridents and they were all full-size. Squidoo tossed in the white bucket.

Rainbow was severe, "You ride in that home. It was a lot of trouble to rescue you."

Squidoo's mouth hole curved and her eyes filled with salty water. "Thank you, twins! Is my party on for tomorrow?"

"The guest of honor, the birthday squid is back!" sang out a happy Bowrain.

"I won't stray again."

"Oh, yes you will," said Rainbow from long personal experience, "but you must tell us where you are."

"You know who you sound like?" asked Bowrain.

"Glendora," said Rainbow. "Hard to believe…"

In the Coral Castle, Glendora was peering into her silver basin at the Aquarium. Humans gazed with disbelief at the empty tank. "Someone took it," said a young woman worker. "I hope they know how to care for squids. They don't do so well in captivity."

A little human boy rubbed tears away. "I wanted so much to see a real squid." "We have some film from yesterday," she comforted him, "come this way."

Glendora turned from the basin, annoyed at her missing children, when the mer twins, holding the bucket with Squidoo, swam into her chamber. "That was risky," she began.

"Daring," said a voice behind her. And there was Neptune, shrinking his huge shoulders to fit into the bedchamber. "Next time, leave a note!"

Rainbow flushed from her waist to the tips of her multicolored hair.

Her father continued in a kinder voice, "All's well now that you're back. Squidoo can have her celebration."

Neptune cradled Squidoo in the huge curve of his gigantic arm.

"You, my dear, are as precious as any creature in my kingdom. " Gently, he rocked her to sleep, then arranged her tentacles half-in half-out the scooped out pond in the twin's room.

"You, my children, he addressed the mer twins, are as noble as any children of the Gods. I applauded your heart and wits; and now your judgment. Even I was a youth once. When I met that nymph, your mother life changed…."

His chuckles echoed down the hall, mirrored in Glendora's amused greeting before the soft sound of the privacy door closed it off.

"Do you think Squidoo will find her mother tomorrow?" asked Rainbow.

"I don't know, but Dad must have some idea. He was keen on the party." And with images of tiny Tridents and giant squids, the twins drifted to sleep in their floaty beds.

CHAPTER 11

Progress reports, presents and Squidoo's celebration

Neptune looked at his family gathered around the conference room in the Coral Castle. He had called this meeting now because this was the time, though he had been ruminating about it for eons.

Again his chart with the caves was on the wall screen, but instead of X's on the bad caves, there were glowing starfishes. They smiled slowly, a circular movement of their legs, that only starfish can make. Neptune looked around him at the dear faces of his family, happy to begin this particular meeting.

"When last we met, I gave out assignments. Today, we have progress reports. And awards," he added barely containing his amusement. His eyes twinkled with mischief, knowing how surprised his children would be. They always thought of him as severe, but in truth, he was a softie. (He didn't find the idea displeasing.)

Glendora raised a questioning eyebrow, though of course she intuited his real purpose.

"Sapphire Onyx is first in our discussion, for whom but Sapphire, alongside Glendora, keeps our home waters happy? She's made her garden into a place of care and refuge for creatures and a source of refreshment. We thank her for helping others to flourish, including us!"

Glendora held up a beautiful hand, "May I mention how her garden has been enjoyed by us all? The dew cakes and seaweeds, the carp berries every day. Thank you, Sapphire!"

Neptune sent a cobalt blue bottle spinning down the table toward Sapphire. Made of translucent glass, smoothed by the ocean, it was pleasant to see and touch. Sapphire opened the stopper and scent wafted over her. Quickly she put the stopper back. "Don't want to waste it!"

"This scent replenishes itself." said Neptune proudly. It's made from wind, water and salt on the most beautiful day imaginable. I captured this for you."

Sapphire anointed her skin and scales, poured fluid down her electric blue hair, until Emerald wrinkled her nose. "Really, Sapph, perfumes can have the opposite effect if you use too much!"

"You stink," Rainbow chimed in.

Sapphire chose to ignore her sisters. She closed her eyes, enjoying the smell and feel of the eternal perfume.

"Next," Neptune began, when he felt a tugging at his tail. There was baby Ruby, shyly gazing up at her father and pointing to Emerald Onyx.

"I was just getting to her. Don't you worry, Ruby."

A clear bell, tiny with a light but insistent sound interrupted this time. He opened his huge hand on the table and a miniscule weight swam in—Pinky Onyx.

Though the Onyx group looked, she was not so visible in Neptune's hand. When they listened, loud and clear, she spoke in mer minds of her love for her step-sister, Emerald Onyx.

"Emerald finds Ruby when she gets lost, and keeps me from being eaten or drifting too far away. She helped me meet my mother and sisters, through a most difficult journey. Emerald is adventurous, brave, patient and very kind! Even when Ruby is demanding and I go my way, she does what she must without lording over us. Size is not the issue, she never bullies and often saves, I applaud her!"

Neptune opened his hand, which was making a clapping sound, as his tiniest daughter swung between his fingers. She beamed, as the whole family was at attention. Her unspoken Mer voice filled the entire conference room. "Emerald's award should be what she never asks for, a time away from us, in a place that delights her."

Emerald, embarrassed, twisted her long green hair and protested. "I go to many places in my music. May I play my song-poem about how different travel in your body is from travel in your mind?"

She found a jellyfish harp willing to have its extremities plucked, and sang in the lyrical storytelling Mer of their tradition. Here was Sapphire's meeting with Charlie in Coney Island, and their idyll in the New Jersey swampland with lobsters and crabs. The encounter of Mermaid and human boy was a meeting and distancing of spirits in harmony and opposition. It was love that could not be, yet remained, beautiful and strange.

Sapphire, of course, glared at her sister for making her

secret into a song. But if her parents were upset about it, they never said. After all, she comforted herself, she and Emerald were sixteen. She had been unconventional but it was a time to be so.

Glendora kissed Emerald. "Oh wise child, you do have our gift. I will give you a tool for knowledge. You may need a lifetime to learn how to use this." With that Glendora handed Emerald her silver basin. "Keep track of us and tell me what you see."

Clearly mom's favorite, thought Rainbow. "Hard to keep track of my traveling twins," said Neptune.

"Time traveling," added Glendora, gazing meaningfully at Bowrain and Rainbow. "Our kingdom needs its bards, like Emerald, who entertain us with what they see."

"We also need explorers" Neptune continued. "Rainbow and Bowrain have done us service at no little risk. Thanks to the fates you two balanced each other. Between Rainbow's rash risk-taking and Bowrain's slower careful thinking, great teamwork happened. You met the challenge, and then some!" Neptune's grin was a knowing one.

Bowrain flushed a pink deeper than Ruby's tail. Rainbow happily bathed in her father's approval. "Your adventures will be celebrated in our family's lore and Mer beyond." Neptune finished, a proud arm around each twin.

"Don't forget Squidoo!" said the twins at once. "We rescued her. That's not over."

"Not yet," He said softly to them. "You also rescued yourselves, quite a few times," he began louder to the assembled. "In the process, you explored quite a few caves. I've put them on a new map. It is yours," he said handing Rainbow a scroll. You are our Ambassadors to parts unknown."

"Bowrain, a tool for future investigations, "

Neptune slid down the table a pair of tiny binoculars that became hand-size, as they reached Bowrain. When he looked inside, he saw the shifting landscapes of different continents.

"You can see anywhere in the world," said Neptune. "Pick a place," said Rainbow excitedly, "Any place!"

Bowrain looked at the maps on the wall. Quick as thought, he found himself viewing a desert, a jungle, a strange ocean.

"I haven't forgotten you, my Rainbow," said Neptune. Down the table he sent two items: a fish tail that went over her regular one and an old rusty, cracked mirror. He was surprised by her disappointed expression. "Out of the stormy black mood, please!" he admonished her, though secretly, he thought, *this daughter is the most like me in moodiness! How have I been so blessed?*

Dad doesn't think much of me, went Rainbow's dark thought.

"Put on the fins and look in Emerald's basin," said Neptune. "Find a place with dry land."

The fins fit Rainbow like another skin. She gazed inside Emerald's basin, thinking of the island Sapphire had visited; the one where humans masqueraded as mermaids. There she was on Coney Island! She came out of the water on human legs!

Then she understood what an amazing resource her father had provided. She could masquerade as a human. The second present she thought was a joke about her vanity, and a shabby one. Well, no other mermaid had such multi-colored hair. What was wrong if she admired it?

She ran her fingers through a strand and looked in the mirror. On one side of the crack was the image of herself at her best. She looked happy. Her hair shined and glowed. Her skin had a starlight sheen. The other side of the crack was a vain pouty mermaid with matted hair and barnacles on her tail. Both needed a good brushing.

Her worst and her best sides? Rainbow was confused. She thought the question to her father, *why this gift?*

Glendora came over and took the mirror from Rainbow and held it up to herself. "All of us think of ourselves as looking one way, while others may see us differently. Depends on the viewer, as well as how the object thinks of herself."

"If I think I'm beautiful and perfect, it will show me that and also that I'm not."

"You will see how you appear to yourself and to others. Much depends on what is in the viewer's mind. Give it to someone else and you'll see what they see."

Rainbow handed the mirror to Bowrain, who gazed at his sister. On one side of the crack was herself in their room, before sleep. She looked like a small Mer child, curled around herself in a circle, tail touching her head.

The other side showed a regal, if somewhat haughty, mer princess.

"I get it," she said. "This gives me more perspective on myself?"

"And other people." said Glendora. "It's the best practice for maturity."

"Who wants to be a grown up," pouted Rainbow. Neptune rolled his eyes, "If you are done, my princess, we have a party to throw!"

Glendora swam over and opened a wall of the Coral Castle. Awaiting the Onyx family was a floating orchestra

GLENDORA *swam over and opened a wall of the Coral Castle. Awaiting the Onyx family was a floating orchestra of squids.*

of squids. They whooshed air bubbles through tentacle oboes and plucked tentacle violins and harps. An audience of squids, from all over the world, enjoyed the music. They ate krill snacks, fed their young, flirted with prospective mates, and wondered when they might see their host, the Great Neptune of Seas.

He raised his arms to the sky, palms together, and brought them down in a straight line. It was a signal for much excited gyration of fluid bodies and inky displays. "May I introduce you to my children, Rainbow and Bowrain, and their young friend, who now belongs among you, SQUIDOO!"

Bowrain and Rainbow came forward with Squidoo. She peered shyly at the assembled squids. Her eyes widened at the crowd. She gasped in great surprise at so many squids, so varied in size and color!

"They are all your family," Neptune calmed her. "Squidoo was lost as a baby and rescued by my children, who raised her until she got too big. An adventurous girl, she swam to human shores and ended up in a wide building which holds water and sea creatures."

All the assembled shuddered, having heard about these places. "But my children found a way to rescue her again! She's back with us like before, but Squidoo is no mer child. She needs to learn to live as a squid. Who among you will be parent and teacher?"

A set of tentacles were raised. "I will do this, Neptune," said a Chinese cuttlefish. "My family would be honored to have Squidoo join us. She would learn the inking techniques of our ancestors."

A greenish gray squid from the Amazon came forward. "We live under the rapids and grow to super sizes. We see no men and greatly enjoy the warming of the earth. Food is plentiful and she will grow to her full size, if something bigger doesn't get her! But that is the way of the Amazon. We have beautiful lives but they can be short. We have many little ones to ensure we are always around."

Two small Scottish black squids from shallows in the North Atlantic came to the front. "See how she looks like us? We have lots of offspring and sometimes they get away from us! We gather close the ones we can. We would be careful Squidoo doesn't lose her way again! She can help us hunt for the little ones."

While Neptune was considering them, a large red squid of unknown origin surfaced. He said, "I will teach you, Squidoo, to avoid predators, enjoy the deep and know when to return to the shallows. You will grow, find a mate, and then have your own Squidoos. I can partner you in this great endeavor."

Squidoo swam to him, happy yet tearful. "You will be my friend." Then the old mother squid, who had tried to help Squidoo at the Aquarium came forward. "I will be your mother, Squidoo, and care for you. I know I am old, but I am wiser than when I was young. I can teach you to find food, avoid capture and care for your young ones. When you are fully grown, I will welcome your mate and my well – deserved repose."

Squidoo looked from the old loving mother squid to the large red squid. She wrapped her tentacles around the old mother. A look of sweet affection passed between them.

Then the old mother said to the large red squid, "Will you come visit us? Squidoo will need some fun company." And the old mother drew the red squid into the multi-tentacle embrace.

Neptune raised his hands, approving Squidoo's choice.

A cacophony of squid sounds ensued, until Emerald took charge with her jelly fish harp. She sang, her harmony transforming all sound to beautiful Mer music. At the end of the celebration, as their guests left, Rainbow and Bowrain sat wrapped in Squidoo's tentacles. The quiet Mertwins were sad she would soon be gone.

"Remember me?" asked Bowrain, as Squidoo detached herself to meet her new family. She turned a happy eye to him and Rainbow and waved her front tentacles. She swam off; a spiral of head and tentacles disappeared in an excited cloud of black ink.

"I liked knowing her. Very different from fish," agreed Bowrain. "A real adventure."

Later, Bowrain and Rainbow were in their room, preparing for sleep. Bowrain picked up their map, "What caves are left, Rainbow?"

She pointed to two with X's. "One of these after school tomorrow?"

Bowrain agreed, and that night, while the rest of the family slept, Bowrain went to the stables with clumps of sea salt.

Boy Boy awakened as Bowrain entered. He neighed and Bowrain swam over. Fondly, he patted the seahorse's muzzle and gave him a clump.

"Adventure?" thought Rainbow.

"Anticipation," Bowrain thought back. *"Planning."*

"After school." said Rainbow. "Don't worry. I have it all worked out.

THE END

Reader's Guide for *Tales of the Mer Family Onyx*

Q. How did you come to write *Tales of the Mer Family Onyx*?

A. The book started as a routine my son and I developed on car trips. My husband's family had a cottage on Long Beach Island, New Jersey and we often travelled there from New York City. In that time, Surgeon General Koop had said no screens before the age of two so on these trips I told stories. My son, a fan of mermaids, wanted us to make up our own. He wanted a dragon in one or a mermaid who would not listen. So over time we evolved a family of them. Around six, he wanted a story where a real mermaid met a fake one at the Coney Island Mermaid Parade. He was in that parade, his skin covered in green make-up carrying a red trident. I wore a vinyl material printed with a coral reef. We walked the boards with others like us.

Q. Did fantasy have a negative impact on your son's adjustment to the real world?

A. I think it enabled him to better understand it. From an early age, he knew there was a division between the oceanic world and ours. He was aware that people polluted nature. There was trash on our beach, dead creatures washed up with plastic, tar stuck to bare feet. Once in Florida, he could not swim in the ocean because of red algae caused by global warming and chemicals. A local radio station doing a story, filmed him, explaining his feelings about red algae.

At five, he knew mermaids weren't real, though he still wanted to meet one. There was no contradiction. Because no one else had met one, didn't mean there weren't any. Fantasy was fluid with reality in his Mer world, until about nine, when the Jersey Devil became more interesting.

Q. Where did the Mer Family members come from?

A. An only child, my son had interest in big families. He thought of Mer folk as females, but liked the idea of a mer boy. So we had boy and girl tweens, Bowrain and Rainbow, rivals and devoted siblings. Like many younger kids, he also admired teens, so we had Emerald and Sapphire, teenagers who wanted to be free from family chores. Neptune had a demanding job and had to travel a lot. He tried to be strict but fair, then was off somewhere. Glendora had the day to day responsibility of her family and though farseeing, she was preoccupied with making sure all was in order. Her kids could resent her supervision, though they depended on her kindness.

Q. Why Onyx?

A. Neptune's fishtail is in the water, while his upper body reaches to the heavens. He's a god, who commands the elements, a conduit between earth and sea. Black Onyx is said to absorb and transform negative emotions. Sorrow can become joy. Onyx is also associated with "healthy egotism." Sounded like Neptune and his family. He arbitrates the variable weather of the gods, the needs of his sea kingdom and the interlopers—mankind. The inverse of Neptune's balance is Anderson's *The Little Mermaid*, who's caught between worlds.

Q Why are there mermaid stories?

A. Many children, and not a few adults, seek to know where they fit in the world. Probably why almost every culture has some version of Mer stories. In some, Mer folk are half human, half water snake instead of fish. This book has invented mermaids, ninjas and minis. I had fun with their devices, shell phones and eel light. I was inspired by the complete worlds conjured by L.Frank Baum's *Oz* and *Sea Fairies* books, as well as E. Nesbit's *The Story of The Amulet* and *The Magic City*. I wanted to have the Mer World both familiar and strange.

Q. What about Ariel?

A. My son knew Anderson's *The Little Mermaid* before he saw Ariel's red hair in the Disney film. He loved the music, lobster friend and Ursula in the movie, but the stories are very different to me. In Anderson, the girl saves her Prince and then sacrifices herself—her individual voice—to keep him and he doesn't know! The tragedy is the girl goes to any length for love, yet her faith is misplaced. They are of different worlds, not to mention races. Love doesn't conquer all, and in Anderson's time, when girls were very limited by class and sex, unbridled passion led to disgrace with no refuge. He gave his mermaid divine grace for her noble heart. Even his sea witch isn't evil but a wise woman, who tries to dissuade her. By contrast, Ariel in the Disney movie is rescued from Ursula by the prince. Unlike Anderson's *The Little Mermaid*, who suffers for her choices, Disney's Ariel is saved by others. She gets what she wants because she's beautiful. In Anderson, being physically beautiful doesn't get her the prince, her voice is an irredeemable loss.

Q. Why do you object to a happy ending?

A. Many fairytales are about transition, the journey of a child who grows up. I think the journey is more important than just how the story ends. Take *Jack and the Beanstalk*. A boy goes to sell his mother's cow at market but only gets beans. And, he must outsmart a fearsome giant to make their fortune. In the original *Beauty and the Beast*, a girl, to save her father, agrees to live isolated from her family with a great beast. Before she can rescue herself and her father, she must tame the beast. To do this, she must learn to see his true character behind his evil looks and appreciate her own value.

Q. What's special about Mer Family?

A This book began as a collaboration between an adult and a young child. We set a family life of parents and kids in a fantastic world. There are dangerous beasts in strange caves and discoveries of beautiful kingdoms and races. In the process, the children grow. The parents, in dealing with their kids, also have to change. I didn't think of writing these down, until my son was past his Mer phase. As Ripley's *Shrunken*

Heads came to dominate our trips, my husband and I found ourselves missing the sweeter world. He suggested I write them down before I forgot them.

Q. What do you hope to give to readers?

Fun, joy, discovery, recognition, sweetness, fantasy, a good night's sleep?

CPSIA information can be obtained
at www.ICGtesting.com
Printed in the USA
BVOW11s1637130517

484055BV00001B/7/P